A Government Countess

A GOVERNMENT COUNTESS

A NOVEL OF DEPARTMENTAL LIFE IN WASHINGTON

BY

MARTHA LEMON SCHNEIDER

(Mrs. Charles W. Schneider)

NEW YORK AND WASHINGTON
THE NEALE PUBLISHING COMPANY
1905

To My Husband

CHAPTER I

RALPH DENNISON ran lightly up the wooden steps leading from the tunnel-like depot of the Baltimore and Ohio Railroad, at Washington, D. C., one lovely spring evening in the year 187—. Seeing a policeman resting against the frail wooden railings at the head of the steps, he inquired of him the way to the National Hotel.

On being told it was a short way off, he determined to walk. Having traveled all day, he was glad of a chance to stretch his cramped limbs.

He walked briskly along C street to First, looking only in the direction the policeman had pointed out to him.

He had heard and read so much about the beautiful streets of Washington, and the wonderful improvements being made, that he was disappointed with what he saw, and well he might be if his first impressions were reliable.

The surroundings of a railroad station are seldom attractive, nor would these call for remark were they not at the very gates of the Capitol of a great nation.

Broken-down fences, car-stables, vacant lots adorned with dumpings of tin cans and more harmful refuse, dilapidated shanties, and cheap

7

lodging-houses with their already lighted transparencies, bearing the enticing legend, "Meals and Lodging, 25 Cents"—these were some of the attractions he saw, all covered with the dust and dirt of a great railroad, which, like the serpent in Paradise, trailed its grimy way even up to the Seat of Knowledge. Half lifting its ugly head, it cast defiance upon its lovely neighbor, puffed its thick, black breath against the pure whiteness of its marble sides, shrieked like a million demons through its many windows, clashed its bells and flashed its fiery eyes in bold self-complacency.

But Ralph thought not of this. Like the Members in those marble halls, his eyes were fixed due westward. He looked not to the right or to the left; he saw only the wide, dirty streets and tumbling-down houses before him.

What he saw depressed him, and he wondered if he was to be disappointed in all his expectations. Just as this impression flashed through his mind he turned and beheld the Capitol, crowned with the rays of the fast-departing sun.

The sun was low in the west; golden rays broke through the gathering clouds and tipped the pure white dome with roseate glory. Far below, the city lay in its bed of green, in peace and beauty, the shaded streets becoming dark while yet the air was filled with sunset hues.

Majestic, somber, beautiful, high above the city's tallest trees, it stands upon its knoll of green, with wings outstretched and head well up in the air. Like some gigantic bird, it seems to guard not only the city at its feet, but the whole United States.

Proudly reflecting the departing day, it appeared like an emblem of "Hope." For would not those sunset hues above the dusky pathways seem to say in letters of Eternal Light, "Though I depart, yet will I return"?

Looking on a sight so fair, Ralph felt again the glorious hopes of youth. They quickened his pace and appeared to add lightness to his feet and give buoyancy to the whole sway of the body.

Seen in the soft tints of twilight, Pennsylvania Avenue seemed immense to him.

It was nearly deserted, only a few stragglers hurrying home to dinner or a slowly passing car or quickly driven carriage were to be seen. As he looked across its wide expanse he stepped yet more quickly, as though the width of the street would somehow add to the distance he had to go, and was surprised to find himself in a few minutes in front of the National Hotel.

Ralph had come to Washington to obtain a Government position. With the confidence of inexperienced youth, and a heart full of ambitious plans, he had joined the army of office-seekers, knowing nothing of the magnitude of that army, or the number who are left stranded each year.

Born and raised in a country town, not many miles from New York—near enough, in fact, for that city to exert a strong influence upon his quiet village and absorb, as it did yearly, its best young blood—he had early in life felt the attraction of the great city. "Who, with a spark of ambition, would be content to bury himself in its peaceful sleep?" he would say of his native town, as he longed for the more active life of the outside world.

Thus, year after year, the village lost its choicest blossoms, and were it not for the world-worn travelers, seeking a quiet spot to end their tired lives, or raise their young away from the evils of a large city, it would indeed have become a "Sleepy Hollow."

Just when it first dawned upon him that the village was too small for him, that as soon as he could he would go out into the world to seek his fortune, he could not remember. While yet a mere lad, he would run through wood and tangled bramble up to the steepest hill-top from where he imagined the city could be seen, dim and gray in the distance; but, like the gold at the end of the rainbow, it was beyond his reach.

As he grew older his desires assumed more definite form, and the determination to leave home took a firmer hold upon his life.

When his father, who was one of the village merchants, took him from school and put him to work in the store, he was, in a measure, happy. Not that he loved work better than study, but that a part of each week's salary put carefully in a little box meant "away."

His father, a slow, easy-going man, satisfied

with the day's plenty, could not understand the boy's longing. The mother, who idolized him, could not bear the thought of him leaving home.

Still, the purpose remained firm within him, and he waited only until he could say to his father, "I am going to seek my fortune."

When the spark of ambition had once ignited the soul, fuel was not wanted to keep the fire going.

He had one friend to whom he told his plans, who helped to fan the flames. This was the village postmaster, "The Judge," as his friends called him. He was the one energetic spirit in the whole place; energetic in making others do, in planning other people's lives; energetic as to what should be done and what should not, for others; who should run for petty offices; and who would have managed the whole Government, if he could have done so by talking. A man with energy enough for the whole village, but none for himself; who could talk and plan for everyone's interests but his own. Years ago he had been made postmaster by a grateful friend who had secured a big "plum" by his aid, and there he seemed to rest, satisfied with this honor and the little law business of the village.

Perhaps, after all, he was right; there he reigned supreme, his little band of followers were staunch and true. Perfectly independent and free, he served out his advice to all, and took none from any. If the world outside the village knew him not, unless through the "Blue Book," he never seemed to know it; his belief in his influence was fixed.

He talked so much of how the Government should be run, and as his party was then in power and nearly always successful he attributed that success to be a part of his own doings. With an ambitious boy, what cannot such a man do? He took a keen interest in all the youths of the village, from the time they came in petticoats until they grew to have opinions of their own; then woe to them if they differed from him—he could then see no good in them.

While yet a rosy, laughing-faced boy, he singled out Ralph as a special favorite, and it was not long before he knew of his ambition—if, indeed, the ambition's sprouts were not all of his own planting. The soil was ready, and the "Judge" cast his seeds right and left.

The post-office was the lounging place of the village, the headquarters of all the news, and there Ralph loved to linger, too young to take an active part in the discussions, but a fervent listener to all that was said. It was there his hopes and plans of getting out into the world finally matured, and the current of his life changed.

He was nearing his twenty-first birthday, and he intended upon that eventful day to declare his intention of leaving home. He had been undecided as to where he should go. He had made any number of plans, had built many castles, but had come to no decision as to just what he should do. He would go first to his uncle's in the city,

and there look around him. He had no fear but
that he could get plenty to do, and he was willing
to work if it was only congenial work. He de-
spised weighing out sugar and serving out lard.
Seoner or later he would get into politics; that
was the only settled idea he possessed.

It was about this time that he found his objective point.

CHAPTER II

ALL the woods had blushed at Autumn's kiss.

From the river banks up to the narrow ledge of rocks upon which the village was built, there arose abruptly a mass of vivid color like a Persian mantle hung before the portals of some gigantic temple.

Back of the few narrow streets which constituted the village arose another curtain of exquisite autumn tints, lost in the blue of a November sky but little brighter than the river below.

The long row of houses, as seen from the river, appeared like children's play-houses set upon a high shelf.

The principal street skirted the edge of the precipice, and was intersected half way by the only road to the mountain-top, following the course of a wild mountain stream, which babbled down the wide mountain-side to fall in wondrous beauty over the steep descent to the river. It was just where the lovely stream prepared to leap into the river's arms that the village post-office stood. It was there the "Judge" had his home; nor could it have been better located for him to see all the coming and going of the village. Did the

14

mountaineers come down to the village, or the villagers go up to the mountain, they must pass his door.

Here was also located the busiest and noisiest part of the village, and above all was the tumult of the stream.

There had been an election and success had crowned the "Judge's" candidate, and his bland "Horace Greeley" face seemed broader and rounder than ever.

His spectacles were set back on his bald head; his round, owl-like eyes appeared to gain brightness by their removal; but over the short, stout body there seemed to creep the fatigue of over-exertion. He was no longer the energetic speaker of a few days previous, when he could have been seen any hour in the day "waylaying" all who passed his door, and "talking up the vote" of his candidate. Now was his time for rest; he had succeeded, and was therefore happy, if tired out. Having given forth a number of "I told you so's," etc., he had pulled up his easy chair, and taking out his pipe, was enjoying his laurels. The usual loungers were there, and Ralph on his favorite stool. Nearly all present were elated over the "great affairs of State," for those who were not in sympathy with the Republican party did not love to linger there.

"Any mail for me, 'Judge'?" said a voice from the open doorway. All turned to look at the man who had appeared among them. He was tall and stout, with rather a handsome face, upon which an easy good nature and unemotional life had left only lines of mirth and indolence.

In fact, he seemed to lack the necessary effort to bring his whole body within the room, as only one foot rested upon the doorstep, while the other remained upon the ground, as though the muscles of his legs had said, "Why raise the body until we know there is something in the room for the master?"

"Well, I should say there was," replied the "Judge." "Reach that bundle down, Ralph. I am too dead tired to move."

Ralph quickly took down a large package of official letters and documents, all bearing the postmark of Washington, and handed them to the "Judge."

"What do you think of the election, Jim?" said the "Judge," as the owner of the package came forward slowly to get it.

"Oh! that's all right," he replied, with little interest in the matter, all he seemed capable of feeling being given to the package in his hand.

"Well, you are a great Government clerk," said the "Judge." "It's a wonder they don't put you out down there. Here you've been drawing salary for fifteen years from our party, and this is the first time you have been home to vote for that party for five years, and I expect your coming this time is owing to that sweet little bride you have with you. You must be thought a great deal of at the Department to be retained as long

as you have been. Pretty important position that
of yours, Jim, eh ?"

Jim's face was a study as he had examined the
package of letters and papers. There was suppressed amusement struggling with the desire to
seem important. Importance gained the control
at the "Judge's" last question.

"I should say it was," said he; "that is the
reason I have not been home for so long. They
can't spare me. I expect this is from the Secretary about a subject we were discussing before I
left," and he held out an official document
franked "Secretary's Office, Department of the
Interior," and addressed to the "Hon. James
Donovan." A dozen necks were craned to get a
look, and pangs of envy shot through as many
breasts. "I should not be a bit surprised if I
have to go back now before my leave is out," he
added, and, taking a handful of Government
rubber bands from his pocket, he carefully as-
sorted his papers; then, with an air of the utmost
importance, put the letters and smaller documents in his pockets, and, gathering up the
papers and pamphlets to the best of his ability,
turned to leave the office.

"These letters will need an immediate reply,"
he said as he passed through the door.

Jim's roguish eyes took in the whole group
there, and he saw the jealousy and envy plainly
written on some faces, the open admiration upon
others. His air of importance and braggadocio
were well assumed.

He had at first been surprised at the size of his
mail; but he soon understood it. "The boys" at
the office had thought it a good joke to shower a
lot of old speeches and dry statistical matter upon
him, knowing what little reverence he had for
such things. Seeing the effect the mere sight of
the papers had upon his fellow-countrymen, he
availed himself of the opportunity to turn the
joke upon them. When he returned to the office
he would surprise the boys by telling them of the
good turn they had done him by giving him this
chance to magnify the importance of his position
at Washington.

This was not the only effect of the joke, however. As one who, year after year, attends a bud-
less plant with watchful care, loving it only for
the fresh, green leaves, awakens in the night to
find the perfect bloom and the air laden with
its intoxicating sweetness, and is thrilled with the
pleasure of a promise fulfilled, so was it now
with Ralph.

In the course of fifteen minutes his plans were
matured and finished. He no longer doubted
what he should do. It is true he mistook the bud
for the bloom; as quick as the thought came it
seemed as though his object was already accomplished. "Why had he never thought of this before?" he asked himself. Of course, a Government position at Washington was the very thing.
As Jim left the post-office he was followed by
Ralph, in haste to set the ball rolling. Now, Jim

had noticed Ralph's eager face and was not much startled when he joined him and asked abruptly:

"What is the best way to obtain a position in Washington?"

"Have plenty of influence, my boy."

"Influence?" said Ralph, not taking in the full meaning of the word.

"Yes, 'Omnipotent Influence,' the moving power of this glorious Government. It moves one man out and another in. It persuades high and low to act upon its suggestions. One day it smothers you with roses and the next it fills you full of pins. If you can get enough of the right kind you may be President some day, young fellow."

There was a puzzled look upon Ralph's face, more at Jim's tone and manner than at his words. He had not spent so much time with the "Judge" not to be somewhat familiar with this great power. He had looked upon it as something highly respectable, hard to obtain, but nowise questionable. Jim's manner somehow put it in a different light to him. This was more an impression than a thought, for his mind was too full of his own plans to give much time to anything else.

This much, at least, was accepted. It needed influence. This he felt to be true, and the next question showed he had accepted this as a fact.

"Having influence, how should one go about using it?"

They had by this time reached the drug store,

and the full blaze of light fell upon Ralph's face. It was illumined with eagerness and hope.

He seemed indeed a youthful Apollo, eager for the chase. His eyes were full, far apart, and blue—frankness and truth in every glance; the nose classical in form, the mouth full but finely curved. Tall, slender, straight, with almost the flush of a woman upon his cheek, and with the unsullied light of a pure life beaming from every feature.

Jim turned and looked at him as he asked the above question. The light, satirical manner changed, the bantering mood was gone.

"Great Scott, boy, you don't think of getting a Government position, do you?"

"Why not?"

"Open a peanut stand, take a cart and peddle bananas, but leave 'Government pap' alone. It is poisonous, my boy; it is worse than the opium habit. It will absorb all your energy, kill all your self-respect, and turn you into a parasite of the worst description."

As Jim finished this sentence, the door of the store opened, and two of Jim's friends joined him and thus put a stop to their conversation.

Ralph, feeling himself in the way, soon said good-night. Jim, having been stirred for a moment from his easy-going mood, took Ralph's hand and said:

"Come to see me, Ralph, and I will talk you out of that notion of yours."

Ralph walked slowly home, pondering many

things, but thinking mostly of Jim's last remark.
Could this be the same man he had seen and
heard such a little while ago in the post-office?
Ralph could hardly believe it. A man holding,
as he had done for years, a good paying position
under the Government, who had so lately bragged
of his close communications with the Secretary,
whose mail alone showed the importance of his
position! What could he mean by such words and
earnest manner? Could they be true? He would
see Jim in the morning and find out his true
meaning.

Was the bloom of a night fading? Perhaps;
but Ralph had tended it too long to let it per-
ish. Having once seen the flower, its beauty
could never be forgotten. Jim's words were like
the chill air from an open window. It must be
closed, the plant protected; and, see! there is not
only one, but every leaf bears perfect bloom. He
might, indeed, be President. He smiled as he
recalled those words, and, so smiling, sank into
a peaceful sleep.

Ralph did not see Jim on the morrow, for the
morn brought a sorrow to his home. His father
was stricken with paralysis and lived but a few
days, and by the time he was able to attend to his
own affairs Jim was back at his desk at Washington.

Mr. Dennison had lived only for the day and
died with coffers empty, and Ralph, like the good
son he was, put all personal thoughts from his
mind and turned his attention entirely to the

store. There were his younger brother, his two
sisters and, most of all, his dear mother to think
of. Thus passed two years, not quickly to him,
for he never overcame his dislike to his work; but
harder than all to endure was the monotony of
the village life. Still, they were busy, useful
years, and added not only strength to his character, but also strength to the old purpose.

Things had changed but little in the village,
and but for the small, golden mustache of which
he was the happy possessor, he had changed but
little outwardly.

"Why should he remain in the village?" he
asked himself at the end of these two years. His
brother was now twenty-one, better at the business than he, and perfectly satisfied with it. It
was not large enough for two. He felt himself a
drag, taking from instead of being a help to his
family. His brother could do all, and better
without him. Why not make a break? Thinking over his old plans, the last bright dream
seemed the best.

The impressions of Jim's words were nearly
forgotten, except that it needed influence, and he
therefore set about getting this desirable possession under the "Judge's" tuition.

There was a letter from his minister as to his
high moral standing. There were several strong
ones from prominent residents of the village; also
one from a retired politician, upon which he
placed many hopes, and looked upon with much
pride, for had not the "Hon. Sir" held many im-

portant offices? Of course, he had one from his
Member which the Judge had gone to great trouble to obtain; last, but not least, in Ralph's estimation, the all-powerful one from the "Judge."

What could he wish more? Armed with these
he marched upon the Capitol.

CHAPTER III

SPRING, with her genial presence, smiled upon the lovely city of Washington. The lawns and parks had laid aside their robes of white and decked themselves in loveliest green, long before the woods and fields surrounding the city dreamed that she was near; for in the parks there are no dead remnants of last year's vegetation to mar the warmth of her approach, and when she is here she notes this response and seems to nourish the shrubs and flowers with her tenderest care.

The rows and rows of young, green trees so recently planted, how beautiful they were, decked in palest green!—the tulip, horse-chestnut, locust, laden with tender blossoms. At all times these "green citizens" are things of beauty, not only in spring, but in mid-summer, when the thick, green foliage affords shade for man and beast; in glorious autumn, even after the leaves have all been cast aside, and we see the graceful symmetry of the branches; in winter, when they weave their purple lace-work on the mesh of snow and ice, and the crystal branches sing their song of winter's chilly reign, and snap their icy strings, or shake off the heaped-up snow, which sparkles as it flutters down like gems from worlds above.

To thoroughly enjoy the beauties of spring

24

one must live "near to nature's heart"; but if one must remain in a city at such a time, how fortunate if it be such a garden city as Washington, with its many parks, its beautiful lawns, its lovely vistas, its green-edged streets—Washington, the emerald crown of America. Thus thought Jean Ainslie as she stood among the trees and flowers in Franklin Square one lovely spring morning on her way to her work at the United States Treasury. Neat, trim, dainty, with an earnest, intelligent face, quiet, gentle manners and a sympathetic nature, she met the emergencies of life cheerfully and bravely. Leading the monotonous life of a Government employe, finding light and beauty in darkest shadows, she welcomed with fullest joy the coming of spring. Often, as she noted the first signs of the sap in the fresh, young grass, she thought that each blade as it broke the soil was like the dawn of thought timidly looking into the mind's sunshine, and to her the "buds and tiny leaves seemed emblematic of youth's imperfect language which time and cultivation would mould into masterpieces."

Due at the office at nine, she allowed herself time for strolling through the park, now stopping at some shrub to smell its sweet perfume or note the bursting buds upon some stately tree; admiring the golden forsythia bushes with their branches of summer sunshine, the scarlet and rose Japan quinces, the soft tint of the lilac, and the snow-balls and the syringa, as the days grew warmer, and in summer the symmetrical designs with summer flowers and gem-tinted leaves.

Even in winter the park held its charm for her, for the snow and ice gained new beauty as it draped the trees and sparkled on bush and shrub. Well did old Samuel, the gardener, know this gentle maiden, and many a dainty flower he gave her which she treasured all day at the office and carried home to brighten her little room at night. To-day, it was the tulips which held her longest on her way. What vivid splashes of crimson; what bold dashes of purple; such darting rays of yellow and gold springing up out of the dark earth, which but a few days ago seemed a barren spot, bearing on their slender stalks all the colors of nature's palette for "Flora" to tint the flowers of summer. How proudly they stood in their rich beauty, standing apart, each in its little bed of green, each feeling itself a queen of spring.

Jean felt their beauty, and if their heads were held up so erect as to win the admiration of the passer-by they received it from her.

But it would not do to linger too long, so, stepping along briskly with the brightness of the spring morning on her sweet face, she was soon within the long halls of the Treasury. Tripping lightly up the broad granite steps, she was quickly before the large iron doors which then protected the Bureau of Engraving and Printing from the outside world. Nodding brightly to the short, stout keeper of the gates, she passed on to the long room beyond. This room was nearly

square, the ceiling low and the light poor, the
sunshine of this bright spring morning but feebly
coming in through the three low, barred windows,
situated as they were under the projecting roof
which never allowed the sun to penetrate far into
the room.

The atmosphere was stifling, and filled with an
odor of freshly printed paper and the oil of machinery. The windows were closed, as is usual
in a Government office. They opened like case-
ments, nearly from floor to ceiling, and therefore
could not be opened without raising the "window
war," a battle of which was fought each day.

"Do open the window," said one; "I am suffo-
cating."

"Pray, do not," said another; "it blows on my
neck." Or, "It gives me rheumatism," cries a
third.

Still it goes on, all becoming sensitive and
sneezing at every breath of fresh air, or drooping
and fading without it.

There were two doors in the room, one at the
north, one at the south end, both leading to rooms
just as crowded and close, but with more heavy
machinery.

Across the room, from east to west, with only
a passageway between, were two long tables with
chairs for about forty. Along these tables messengers were placing packages of unfinished
paper money to be counted and examined by the
lady counters. Each package was securely tied
with strong twine, and bore the name of those

who had last worked upon it plainly written
upon the paper label.

These packages of "greenbacks" were brought
by two messengers into the room in long trunk-
like boxes with handles to each end, and were
unlocked by the superintendent, who kept an account of every package taken from the boxes received by her. Packages were placed upon the
tables in front of every alternate chair, as two
counters worked upon each package, and the day's
work was piled up on another long table that
occupied one end of the room, while the desks of
the superintendent and her clerks were at the
other.

There was a general bustle throughout the
whole room. It was nearly full of ladies, most
of them talking and moving about—some taking
off their wraps, others putting on aprons, while
quite a group of them stood around a sink with
little glass cups in their hands containing
sponges; others were waiting their turn at the
sink to wet their sponges or carrying their cups
to their seats by the table.

There had been a wedding, the night before, of
one of their number, and criticisms of those who
had witnessed it were most to be heard.

As Jean joined this group to wet her sponge,
after having taken off her hat and coat and
donned a neat white apron, she was addressed by
one of the young ladies.

"I suppose you will have the new "countess"
for your partner, Miss Ainslie."

"Is there a new one ?" said Jean.

"Yes," she replied, "and she is a beauty. Mrs. Graham will have to look out for her swains."

"Indeed she will," said another.

"If she is so good-looking," observed a third with a sneer, "she will not remain a counter of other people's money long."

At this they laughed, and, the bell ringing for work, hurried to their places.

"Miss Ainslie," said Miss Temple, the superintendent, "will you step here ?"

Jean walked up to her desk, which was at the north end of the room, with a smaller desk on each side of it, and one quite close to the door leading to the back room.

Miss Temple was short and stout, brisk, animated and intelligent, a thorough business woman, filling her position with credit to herself and to her sex. Beside her stood a young girl, tall, slender, beautiful. She reminded Jean of the gorgeous tulips she had so lately admired.

"Miss Ainslie," said Miss Temple, "this is Miss Dora Hart. Will you instruct her in her duties ? She will take Miss Fay's place," referring to the young lady who had been married, and who had been Jean's co-partner.

"I shall be pleased to have Miss Hart for a partner," said Jean, looking at her lovely face.

The new "countess" (for thus the counters called themselves) did not appear shy or embarrassed, although her face was flushed and the lovely mouth compressed, with chin well up in air.

Jean took her to the seat next her own at the end of one of the long tables. She quickly untied the string of the package in front of them, which contained banknotes, four on a sheet, one thousand sheets in a package, separated into hundreds by a long narrow strip of white paper. Jean showed her how to bend the upper right-hand corner, and, moistening her finger on the wet sponge, count and examine the sheets. As she reached the strip of white paper, she would hand the hundred to Dora, who, reversing the corners, counted and examined the other half of the sheet, stacking them up in front of her until the thousand were counted and examined. Then their names were signed and the package removed to be strongly tied up by the messengers. The work was monotonous, but it required a certain amount of skill and nimble fingers to excel.

Since the ringing of the bell for work, all was still; not a sound was heard but the quickly turned sheets and the clicking of the machinery in the room beyond. They were not allowed to talk—although this rule was often broken by low whispering—and were kept supplied with work by silently moving messengers.

Old and young; widows with husbands and without; maids blooming and sere—all plainly but neatly dressed; for a counter's pay is small compared with that of clerks—each swiftly counting money for the millions. No matter how empty their pockets, how much they might need a five-dollar bill, it was phantom money to them, and satisfied none of their wants, and they soon came to regard it as nothing but paper.

I have said "all were busy"; but every hive must have its drones, and this busy workshop had its quorum.

It was half-past nine when Mrs. Graham walked into the room to take her seat at the desk by the door. She was of fine physique, tall and handsome. Her eyes were gray and cold; her mouth full, inviting, tempting. Could one cover the eyes they might enjoy the kiss; and surely she knew this, for the lids with their long lashes were nearly always drooped over the eyes when she wanted to be especially winning. Her hair was of the palest brown, abundant almost to excess. She was dressed always in exquisite taste; the color of her gowns was quiet in tone, but they were expensive as to material and finish. It is true that her salary was large; so was her influence—that supreme power in Washington.

With influence and a big salary (the one is synonymous with the other) life in Washington is paradise. Influence allowed Mrs. Graham to come late without being docked, to do little work and draw large pay, to lounge on the sofa in the dressing-room, and leave early in the afternoon.

Could the hard-working counters look upon Mrs. Graham without envy? Could they work with aching eyes and tired arms, and not long for influence? Nor was it strange that, when oppor-

tunity to gain influence presented itself, as it
frequently did, they fled like the moth to the
light, even if they singed their wings.

Mrs. Graham opened her ledger and appeared
to work, but only for a little while. Her desk
was near the door, and it really was surprising
how many of the male clerks had business which
necessitated stopping at her desk as they went to
and fro through the room.

And so the morning passed, until the whistle
blew for twelve and the half hour for luncheon.
The employes of the Bureau of Engraving and
Printing are not allowed to leave the building
without permission, so nearly all brought their
lunch. There was a pushing back of chairs—
paper weights were put on unfinished work—and
a general moving toward the sink to remove the
poisonous green stain of the "filthy lucre."

"Miss Hart," said Jean, "will you come with
me over in the corner and eat your luncheon ?"

She acquiescing, they joined a few of the
"cold-air Christians" in the corner by the last
window, which they had opened.

The air was balmy with the softness of spring,
but to their over-heated lungs it seemed cool; so,
throwing shawls and wraps around them, they
spread out their luncheon on their laps.

It is needless to say that most of the conversation was of the wedding, and as Dora knew nothing of it, she had little to say. She was seated
on the wide, low sill of the window, looking out,

her fingers woven in between the iron network put there to prevent papers being blown out.

Opposite, the White House was plainly seen through the trees, with their tiny leaves of vivid green and the fresh, young grass at their feet. The fountain sprang gaily in the sunshine, and the chattering sparrows fluttered in and out of its glittering spray.

To the south the river, like the yellow sash of some fair "April's Lady," moved slowly on; while to the north the bustle of a city street could be seen, with its background of grass and trees in the park beyond.

It was a fair view to meet the eyes, and seemed to say:

"Come walk with me; all nature's glad to-day."

Dora seemed to feel this, for almost involuntarily she stood up.

"I feel as though I were in prison," she said.

"It is a prison to most of us," said one of the ladies, "and I made up my mind last night that the only way out for me is through matrimony, and woe betide the unhappy man who gives me a ghost of a chance."

"Oh, I thought you were waiting for a millionaire," said another.

"So I have been; but I say now, with the old maid, 'Anybody, oh Lord!'"

"I hope I shall not come to that," said Dora, with a smile.

If she had been beautiful before, she was bewitching when she laughed, showing lovely dimples and perfect teeth.

"I am sorry, Miss Forest," said Jean, addressing the young lady who had so openly expressed herself in favor of matrimony, "to hear you express a sentiment which betrays one of the principal barriers in the progress of women workers."

"Pray, how is that ?"

"Why, because so few women take up work as a permanency; they do what they have to do always with the hope of getting out of it soon, instead of making it a life object, as men do."

"Horrors !" cried several; "work here for life ?"

Just then the bell sounded, and all hurried to their seats to work steadily until four o'clock.

CHAPTER IV

"Washington, D. C., March 1, 187—.

"DEAR MAY: I have delayed writing to you until after my first day's experience as a working girl, and I tell you right here, I don't like it one bit. I am dead tired, my arms ache, and if my fingers had not been nimbled up by so much piano practice, they would be as stiff as 'Dame Marguerite's' hair we used to laugh so about at school.

"Laugh, did I say? I feel as though I should never laugh again, and if I had not cried my eyes nearly out at the very thought of having to earn my own living in such a way, I should now be weeping and wailing. Instead of being in a melting mood, however, I am furious, outrageously mad with fate.

"Uncle John says I ought to be glad to have so good a place provided for me, and I suppose I ought; but think of the present as it is and as I had planned it.

"It is true I have known for the last two years that I should have to earn my own living, but I expected to do so with my voice; but Uncle John persuaded mama during her last sickness to make me promise never to go on the stage. It was her dying request, and although I gave my

35

word, I will never forgive Uncle John, and that is one reason why I would not accept the home he offered me. I at first thought of taking pupils; but, you know, they live in the country and I know no one in the city.

"Uncle John was speaking to Mr. Lance, the Representative from his district, about me one day, and he obtained me this position. So, behold me a "Government countess," handling millions each day; but when my board and wash bills are paid, I will have about fifteen dollars a month with which to adorn my fairy form, less than the cost of the hats I have been accustomed to wear—I, who used to be the finest dressed girl at school, whose wardrobe was the envy of all. 'Verily have the stars fallen!' 'Fifteen dollars!' Think of it.

"I shall be like 'Mr. Wilfer,' and as such in the future think of me. I shall never be in complete apparel again. The hats will be old when the shoes are new, the change through the entire costume long and lingering.

"I have taken an inventory of my effects. There are dear mama's furs; the muff will save gloves—but then it is spring, and by winter who knows what may happen? Perhaps I may be driven to do what one of the ladies said to-day, 'get married for the sake of a home.' That reminds me that I started out in this letter to tell of my day's experience, but have wandered to my personal woes; but you know your dear old 'will-o'-the-wisp' too well for me to make excuses.

"Well, I am too exhausted to give a detailed account of my day now; but I was put to work counting 'real money,' though not ready for circulation. I had for a partner a sweet little lady, very demure and quiet, but I fear I shall try her very greatly; but, really, I am going to reform. I am going to take her for a model and become a 'plodder.' Perhaps I shall mount the ladder yet. Do write me. I forgot to tell you I am stopping with friends of Uncle John, have a fairly good room, and really intend to be content.

"Give love to all the dear ones with you, and be thankful for your comfortable home.

"Your dolorous friend,

"Dora."

"I wonder what it is like to have a home?" said Dora to herself as she finished her letter, having addressed it to her dearest school friend.

"Perhaps it is just as well I never remember having one, now that I am entirely alone in the world. Let me see," she continued, slowly rocking; "I was two years old when papa died—of course I have no recollection of him, but I do remember living with dear old grandma, who died when I was about six. Yes, that is the only home I remember. I recollect the wide window-sill upon which I used to play with my dolls, and upon which I used to love to sit and watch the people going by to the big factory up the street, and swarm out like bees at twelve and five. I little imagined I would become one of such a multitude. I thought of that to-day as I sat in the window of the office. I wish I did not hate to be pent up in any place."

With this she got up and walked the floor, taking long strides with hands behind her.

"Boo!" she said to herself in the glass as she passed the bureau. "I remind myself of a leopard with my yellow eyes and restless ways."

Taking down her hair and brushing out the soft auburn curls, she continued to review the past.

"After grandma died, mama gave music lessons. I think we were poor. Then mama went upon the stage again. She was an actress when papa married her. She put me to school; there I remained until two years ago, when poor mama lost her voice and became very ill. I nursed her for nearly a year. My beautiful, beautiful mama!"

Tears came to Dora's eyes, and laying down the brush she opened a drawer and took out a large velvet box; opening it disclosed dozens of photographs, each with the same face, but in many poses, many costumes—such pictures as an actress has taken.

Dora took up a handful and looked at them one by one.

"These contain most of my recollections of my mother, and as such I wish only to remember her. The days of her illness are painful to me; but these are as I nearly always saw her from the footlights—smiling, singing, beautiful. Always clapping of hands and enthusiasm. When she happened to sing anywhere near the school she would send for me and I would go with her to the theatre. How I loved it and looked forward towards those days and lived them over for weeks afterwards! How proud I was of her when she came out to school in her elegant clothes and diamonds!—they all went to nourish her in her illness. Uncle John says she was extravagant and spent her money like water. I expect I am like her in that respect. She certainly gave me everything elegant. No one had such presents and clothes as I in the whole school.

"I shall never be as beautiful, I know"; and rising she went to the glass. "I don't look one bit like her, except the dimples," she said. "She was a blonde and I am almost dark."

Dora looked at the face in the photograph and then at her own face in the glass, kissed her favorite picture and sighed, locked them all up in the box again and went to bed to dream of the mother who had been to her rather a beautiful vision than a mother in reality—a mother whom she could remember only with her stage settings and clothes.

And Dora, with her sensuous beauty, wilful disposition, love of dress and admiration; uncontrolled all her life, except by school discipline; alone in Washington, earning her own living—how was she to steer clear of all the quicksands of Department life?

CHAPTER V

WHEN Jean entered her room after her day's work she was met by the sweet notes of two canaries, whose cages hung in a small bay window which was a perfect bower of green shrubs and scarlet geraniums. She answered them with a soft, low whistle, which caused them to flutter and hop, and sing even more wildly than before. Going up to their cages and opening wide the doors, they were soon flying gaily around the room, lighting on some picture frame or ornament to try new notes to express their pleasure.

The room was neat and cheerful, showing in its few ornaments the good taste and love of the beautiful possessed by its occupant. A good water-color copy of Fortuny's "Rare Vase" occupied the most prominent place over the mantel.

Jean felt a strong sympathy for the fat old man in his evident keen enjoyment of his rare vase. Being a true worshipper of beauty in all its manifold forms, she understood the pleasure which such an object might give.

Looking always for something to admire in those she met—sometimes it was a finely formed ear, the hair as it grew around the face or neck, the curves of the nostrils, or some mark of beauty usually overlooked in a plain face—she had been

charmed all day by the beauty of her companion.
She could hardly keep her eyes upon her work, so
bewitched was she by Dora's striking beauty.
Knowing nothing of her, only exchanging a few
words together, yet she felt drawn towards her
by an attraction she could hardly resist, and felt
it would be a pleasure just to have her where she
could look at her and study the many beauties of
her face and figure.

Jean boarded with a former worker who had
been married a little over two years. Having
no home or relation in the city, she was glad
when this little home was opened to her. Mr.
and Mrs. Donovan thought her perfect and
treated her like a younger sister. They had
named their little daughter after her, and this
little darling was one of Jean's chief pleasures
in life.

Having freshened herself for dinner, Jean
gave a low whistle and the two wandering birds
flew quickly onto her outstretched finger, each
pushing and pecking at the other, as though to
shove its rival off that soft, white perch. She
scolded them and put them in their gilded prison
once more and went down to dinner.

She could talk of nothing else during dinner
but Dora, until Mr. Donovan began to tease her.
"She had so much enthusiasm to bestow upon a
pretty face, what would she do when she lost her
heart to some handsome young man?" said he,
and, taking up the *Star*, sat down in his easy
chair to enjoy the news.

Jean took the baby and went into the parlor to enjoy her evening romp with her. Mrs. Donovan, having only a small negro girl to assist her in the housework, began removing the dinner things.

The wife of a Department clerk knows her husband's salary to the cent, and she soon realizes that she must make every cent tell. She cannot indulge herself with things beyond her means, consoling herself with the thought that, "It is the busy season; we can afford this," or, "Business is good now; we can get that," etc.

Mrs. Donovan realized that there were no lucky deals by which to add some luxury, no generous or appreciative master with gifts to tide over, or enable them to pay a debt incurred, perhaps, through the illness of self or little ones. The salary was fixed by the laws of Congress, and when the Government said twelve hundred it meant just so much per month—no more, no less.

It was often hard to endure with patience the fact that her next-door neighbor's husband got sixteen hundred dollars a year for doing exactly the same work that Jim did for twelve hundred; and her dearest friend's husband, who was also in the same division as Jim, got eighteen hundred a year, and everyone knew that he was a very inefficient clerk, but he had the "pull." The leading politicians of his district held high Governmental positions and they were his warm personal friends and strong supporters; he did pretty much as he pleased and much of the work that belonged to his desk was done daily by Jim.

As the salaries of Departmental clerks range from twelve to eighteen hundred per year, and these clerks are all in the same social sphere, it often requires strong self-control on the part of the wives to live within their income, when one can have so many more comforts or luxuries than the other.

Mrs. Donovan had lived long enough in Washington to know that, while the demands of the home increased as the years went on, the salary seldom did, and the only thing for them to do, if they wished to avoid the shipwrecks of which she had seen so many, was to try to save a little while baby Jean was still young and their wants few.

Then there was always hanging over their heads this awful uncertainty of Jim's position. No matter how proficient he might be in his work, there was always the possibility of some superior officer wanting his place for some favorite, or some pressure being brought to bear from the outside, forcing the head of the division to make room for some Congressional appointee.

This uncertainty as to the tenure of his position had kept Mr. Donovan a bachelor for a number of years in which he would say, "he had squandered enough to have given them many comforts now that he was married to the sweetest of girls."

He had, however, escaped being discharged so many times that he had long ceased to worry

about this possibility of his being discharged
without cause. It had the effect of making him
refuse promotion into higher grades when a
superior officer, recognizing his ability, had offered him one, because, he said, "The bigger the
plum the surer the aim." As there are a greater
number of clerks who receive twelve hundred a
year than in the other classifications, he felt that
there was more of a chance that his place might
be overlooked when a search for places was made.

He was fast becoming a mechanical machine
—did his portion of work, the ends and results of
which he never saw. He could make no new ven-
tures, take no risks; his daily work, of which
there was always a plenty, must be done according to set formula over which he had no control.
There were no seasons of depression or unusual
activity, no labor unions to adjust his wrongs.

Jim's kind heart, easy good-nature, cheerfulness and willingness to assist his fellow-clerks,
made him a general favorite, and having lost the
ambition of his youth he had settled down to a
typical Government clerk, faithfully perform-
ing his duty and caring little for the prevari-
cators, the intriguers, the sycophants, which
prior to the civil service wielded a great power
with their cudgel "influence," for in those days
there was no court of appeal before which a
clerk could go to show cause why he should not
be dismissed, and envy and jealousy and such
evils too often worked their will when influence
backed them up.

Jean was in the midst of a gay romp with baby when the door-bell rang. It was rather early for callers, and knowing that Mrs. Donovan and Topsy were busy in the kitchen, and being also aware of Mr. Donovan's aversion to moving when once down with his evening paper, she hurried to the door with baby in her arms, who tightly clasped her around the neck and hid her face in Jean's hair, as a tall young man stepped into the brightly lighted hall.

"Does Mr. James Donovan live here?" he asked, thinking what a sweet picture she made.

Her fair hair, which she usually wore too smoothly brushed, was mussed by the little one's play, and the generally pale face was aglow from exercise and embarrassment. She invited him into the parlor and went into the adjoining room to tell Jim he had a visitor.

When Jim stepped into the room he failed at first to recognize our friend Ralph.

"You do not remember me," said Ralph, a feeling of depression coming over him. He had so long looked upon Jim as a "friend at court," as it were, that he had overlooked the fact that Jim might not have thought of him since that night, two years ago, when they parted at the drug store. But, even while he was making himself known, he felt how natural it was that Jim should not remember him as he did Jim.

Mr. Donovan tried to make up for his lack of memory by a kindly welcome and cordial inquiries about different ones in the village.

Ralph answered all such questions as briefly as possible, for it was not for this he hunted Jim up immediately after his arrival, and as soon as he could he led up to the thought nearest his heart.

"I hurried here as soon as possible after supper to ask your advice," he said, not knowing that supper in Washington, as he knew it, was almost an unknown custom except among a few of the laboring classes. People in Washington breakfasted late, dined late, carried lunch in hip pocket, held high five o'clock tea, or "kettle drums," as they were then called; but supper they knew not, except after a theatre party, or some such "jinks" in high swelldom.

"I suppose you do not remember me speaking to you two years ago about a Government position ?"

Jim recalled the scene at the post-office, and afterwards that eager, boyish face.

"Are you still determined to become a Government clerk ?" he asked. "I think, if I remember rightly, I advised you against it, did I not ?"

"Yes, you did; but the desire to leave the village was too strong for it to have much weight with me. Neither could I understand why you should have expressed yourself as you did, for surely it is not an ignoble object to wish to serve the Government of which every American should be proud"; and Ralph's face beamed with youthful enthusiasm.

Jim felt a return of his own lost youth. He

checked the sarcastic condemnation which arose to his lips.

"I am glad you do not seek a position in the spirit of so many 'hustlers after office,' for the ease and luxury you imagine an official life brings."

"No; I wish to enter political life for the good of my country."

Jim could barely suppress a smile at this, as he added:

"You are making a serious mistake in connecting yourself with the Government here. You have greater opportunities for political life in the quietest of quiet villages than with a position at Washington. You must drop all political opinions and aspirations when your name is entered on the 'Blue Book.'"

But he argued in vain. Ralph had come to Washington to get a Government position, and nothing would turn him from that object.

Jim seeing this, asked about his "influence." This brought on another long discussion. The recommendations which, to Ralph, seemed so strong were lacking in strength to Jim. He at last told him how to go about "booming it up," and then added a piece of advice:

"When you get your position enter immediately into one of the law schools here. When you get your diploma resign your position and go West. Then you can enter politics in the right way, and, I believe, be a success."

Ralph said he would think of it, and the con-

versation turning to other things, Ralph compli-
mented him on his wife.

"Why, you have never seen her," said Jim.

"Did she not open the door to me?"

Jim laughed. "No; that was our friend, Miss
Ainslie. I will call them"; and he went out and
brought them both in, the baby, during the long
talk of the men, having been put to sleep.

After his wife and Jean had been introduced,
Jim could not refrain from laughing and joking
over Ralph's mistake. They were all soon laughing and talking, and thus passed a very pleasant
evening.

On leaving, Jim told Ralph to look upon his
house as his home while in the city and drop in
often. Ralph replied that he certainly would
do so.

CHAPTER VI

AMONG the many things Jim had said to Ralph was, to get his Member to go to the front for him. "If you present your letters in person," he said, "you will be bowed out politely, and your papers filed away in the appointment room to dry-rot." So Ralph was up early the next morning, determined to get his Member to make his appointment a personal matter.

Long before the hour at which Congress convenes, he was entering the rotunda of the Capitol. Magnificent, it seemed to him, with its panorama of pictures and its immense dome. Proudly he stood before each picture, which were works of art to him, in spite of the critics.

Did not each tell its history of heroic action or famous deed, kindling anew his love of country and reverence for its founders and discoverers? He paid them all due homage, and saw no fault in line or color.

From the rotunda he wandered from hall to room, admiring all, and filled with great patriotic pride as a statue of some noted man or picture met his eye. At last seeing the sign, "To the Dome," he began the ascent, mounting with the lightness of youth up the many steps. It was like climbing the ladder of fame, he thought.

"Step by step, he would mount higher," he said
to himself, as he paused for breath upon the balcony under the picture in the dome.

He would be on top yet, he determined,
hardly stopping to still the beating of his
quickly throbbing heart, and never thinking to
look down upon the great men who were crossing
the rotunda below, on their way to the different
houses of Congress, and who would have appeared large physically only in their feet and
legs.

Climbing with renewed vigor the few remain-
ing but steep steps, he was soon on top, looking
over the lovely city and surrounding country.

Not a cloud dimmed the glory of the sun; the
mist of early morning had passed away. On
all sides beyond the city were clearly revealed
historic spots nestling in the young beauty of
spring.

To the north the marble towers of the Soldiers'
Home looked down upon the city, sheltering the
brave souls who gave up youth and health to save
that city and the nation. Had Ralph known
upon what he was looking as he singled out its
pure white turrets, his heart would have telegraphed to it a cheer. It was one of his greatest
sorrows that he had not been born in time to
serve his country during its deadly peril. So
wondering what building it could be, he walked
slowly around the balcony at the feet of the "Goddess" on his tour of inspection.

Neither did he know as he turned towards the

west, and saw a little to the south the white pillars of General Lee's old home, that around that old homestead lay those who had died upon those fields of battle for which he had so often longed.

Passing his eyes quickly over the Virginia hills, he could dimly see historic old Alexandria in the clear air, and, had he a strong glass, the hotel from which Ellsworth tore the Rebel flag, and a little further on the battlemented wall of old Fort Washington.

But no one being there to point out these interesting spots, upon this beautiful landscape, he felt only the exhilarating sensation of his elevated position, and his mind being full of his own aims, with only a passing glance over the lovely scene, he started down to seek his Member, feeling as though he had already succeeded.

He reached the door of the House of Representatives somewhat out of breath. Jim had told him to send in his card by the messenger there. This he did, and was glad of a chance to wait a few minutes to recover from his trip to the dome. He had never met the Honorable Member who represented him in Congress, the "Judge" having gotten the letter for him.

Ralph was trying to construct the most suitable sentence in which to make his request, when the messenger returned and said, "The Member is in committee meeting, and asks to be excused."

Ralph walked slowly up the hall, with disappointment in his face and manner. How many such footsteps have echoed through those marble

halls! No wonder the watchmen at night hear
mysterious noises and peculiar sounds as they go
their rounds.

Where were now the rush and vim with which
Ralph had mounted flight after flight to the top
of the dome? Slowly, meditatively, he walked up
the steps leading to the public galleries of the
House, not even noticing the picture of "Westward Ho!" the most striking of all the pictures.

But by the time he had taken his seat he had
somewhat recovered his composure.

Who was he, to stop the wheels of Government? He would come the next day a little later
in the afternoon. He was willing to wait his
turn, he told himself, and so settled down to
watch the scene below.

The roll was being called in the monotonous
tones of the reader. Members were taking their
seats, or standing in groups, talking and smok-
ing; others seated at their desks, opening their
mail or getting ready their speeches. Pages running to and fro, bringing books of reference, or
placing glasses of water on the prospective
speakers' desks; carrying letters or notes; darting
in and out between the narrow aisles and through
the softly swinging doors like flying shadows of
restless spirits of diminutive men. Ralph remained and listened to speeches from men whose
names are written on the most glorious annals of
our history.

So absorbed did he become that even the pangs
of hunger passed unnoticed. When he finally

left he felt tired and hungry; the rosy tint of
morning had fled, and in its place was a feeling
of dissatisfaction and depression. He would
never reach the heights of the men he had just
listened to, and perhaps never gain the first round
of the ladder.

After a good dinner he shook off this feeling,
and went to the theatre, and in the jolly company
of the "Vokes Sisters" laughed himself into
cheerfulness again.

Early the next morning he had eaten his breakfast and was out on the street, determined to
walk around and see something of the city before
trying to see his Member.

The air was chilly with gathering rain, instead of the warm spring air of the past few days.
There were the penetrating dampness and dull,
lowering sky which made you hunt up your put-
away overcoat and warned you not to put off your
flannels, as you thought you would have to the
day before.

Ralph did not wander around sight-seeing as
long as he had intended. The cold rain which
was falling and the desire to see his Member
drew him towards the Capitol.

He spent most of his time in the Senate, but it
had not the attraction of the House to him, he
being more in sympathy with the bustle and confusion of the latter than with the quiet dignity of
the Senate.

Somewhat late in the afternoon he again sent
in his card, not with the same expectancy of the

day before, but still with hope. This time the card was brought back, with the information that the Honorable Member had gone to one of the Departments on business.

"Do you think he will be back this afternoon ?" he asked.

"No, sir. 'Tain't likely, sir," was the reply.

Ralph unconsciously heaved a deep sigh, for it is one of youth's hardest lessons to wait with patience.

Somehow, he had no further interest in either House or Senate. He walked slowly back to the hotel through the now pouring rain.

How chilly and miserable the dusky room seemed to him! He began to wonder what they were doing at home. He re-read his mother's letter, and was somewhat ashamed of the first feeling of homesickness which passed through him. He would write her a good, long letter, telling her all he had done and seen. In the evening he would go out and talk things over with Jim.

He had not intended seeing him until after he had seen his Member, for he felt that Jim was not in sympathy with him in the matter, and a feeling of pride prompted him to wait until he had succeeded, even a little; but the lonesome feeling and longing to talk to someone determined him. In spite of the pouring rain, he was soon in Jim's cosy parlor and cheered by his hearty welcome. He told of his failure to see his Member; and Jean, seated on a low chair

opposite, knitting a soft, white sacque for baby
Jean, read all the unexpressed disappointment in
his fair young face, and a wish to cheer him arose
in her heart. Ralph, looking toward her as he
spoke, saw the look and felt thankful for the
unspoken sympathy it told.

"You had better give it up," said Jim.

"I have never thought of that for a moment.
I have put my hand to the plow. I cannot so
easily turn back."

His face looked strong with the strength of
renewed determination. But why should Jean
feel a thrill of pride as she watched that look?

"Well, then," said Jim, "I tell you what I
should advise. Don't pester your Member with
any more cards for awhile at the Capitol. He
evidently does not want to see you, or is really
an active worker. Wait a few days, and then go
to his hotel, and try to get him there."

Ralph thought well of this, and, relying more
than ever on Jim's advice, regained his hopeful-
ness, and was soon telling them of his evening
before with the "Vokes Sisters."

"Have you seen the 'Belles of the Kitchen,'
Miss Ainslie?" he asked.

She replying that she had not, he invited her
to go with him the next evening.

Having engaged good seats and purchased a
bouquet for Jean, he presented himself early the
next evening at Jim's, and he and Jean were soon
laughing heartily over the trials of the "Belles
of the Kitchen."

CHAPTER VII

To say that Jean's heart was in a flutter would not express it, she having received but little such attention from any one, and never from so fascinating a source.

Left an orphan at an early age, she had been adopted by an old maid aunt, who supported herself and Jean through her position in the Bureau of Engraving and Printing, where the Government paper money is made. This aunt had led a lonely life until Jean came to brighten it, and although Jean was left alone all day, the evenings were delightful times to both. As Jean grew older she kept house for her aunt on the top floor of a house which was occupied by an old married couple who kept watch over Jean through the day.

When Jean's aunt died, Jean assumed her place at the Bureau, and soon after went to live with Mr. and Mrs. Donovan.

Jean had enjoyed few pleasures such as most girls have in their youth, but had been happy and cheerful, being the fortunate possessor of a contented mind.

Thus, this lightly placing of her hand upon his offered arm, this kind attention of this handsome

young man, filled her with new emotion, sent the
color to her cheeks and tied her tongue.

Not so Ralph. He was used to being a beau,
and also to shy girls. He chatted and laughed,
and Jean soon found herself at perfect ease with
him.

Ralph doubly enjoyed the performance upon
seeing her pleasure and appreciation of it. He
took her to Harvey's after the play, and they ate
ices and cake with the keen relish of youth, and
Ralph felt that life in Washington was more
desirable than ever.

After that evening they became great friends,
and many a pleasant time they had together.

Ralph had plenty of leisure and always felt
better and happier after a chat with Jean. After
having restrained his impatience many times,
Jim at last consented to his going to see his
Member.

"You had better go just after dinner, for no
man likes to be bothered on an empty stomach,"
he said to Ralph; so, timing himself as well as he
could, he started for the Ebbitt, where his Member was living.

Acting under Jim's instruction, he sent in not
only his card, but the letter of recommendation
from the "Judge."

This proved a wise suggestion, for the Honorable Sir would surely not have been at home to
the simple bearer of the card; but after reading
the "Judge's" letter, he remembered that the
"Judge" (of whose power in his little realm he

was well aware) had spoken to him of this young man, and that he had written a letter of recommendation at the "Judge's" request.

So Ralph was ushered into his august presence, and found him seated before a desk strewn with papers and with every appearance of being hard at work. He still held a bundle of papers in his hand as he arose to meet Ralph, and reseated himself before his desk after greeting him. His whole manner was such as to impress Ralph with the idea that he was very busy and to make his call as short as possible. As briefly as he could, Ralph stated his request.

The Honorable Sir, feeling that the quickest way to get rid of this constituent, and at the same time please the "Judge," was to consent, so made an appointment for the following morning.

Ralph was promptly on hand at the hour appointed, and together they went to the Department of the Interior, Ralph having expressed a preference for that Department.

The Secretary received them in his most gracious manner and listened with the greatest apparent interest and attention to their request. He glanced at the papers and said they should have his early consideration. He would "look around him" and Ralph should be notified as soon as he found a place for him.

Ralph thanked him, and, beaming with pleasure, they left the office. He also expressed his gratitude to the Honorable Sir in terms which should have softened that hardened man's heart;

but they did not, for no sooner had he taken leave of Ralph than he hurried back to the Secretary to tell him privately that "he need not put himself out for that young man; he had merely brought him there to get rid of him—office-seekers were such a nuisance."

"So you propose to throw your nuisances on me ?"

"Not at all, not at all, Mr. Secretary, I assure you."

"It seems so from your remarks."

"You misunderstood me; I am in need of this man's vote, and his friends who are interested in him are useful to me. I must seem to help them and him. They can in no way help you, and if you give an order to your messenger he will not be admitted into your presence to further annoy you."

"I do not countenance such conduct—good morning"; and the Secretary turned from him with a look of great displeasure and disgust.

"Good-morning," replied the Member quickly, as he left the room.

The door closing upon the Honorable Sir, the Secretary ordered Ralph's papers to be placed on file, and soon forgot all about them.

Such a scene was beyond Ralph's wildest imagination. He walked elated and felt confident that it was now only a matter of a very few days before his appointment would be made.

It was about this time that he became ac-

quainted with a young lawyer from the West,
who was stopping at the same hotel.

Both being strangers, they soon became friends
and visited many points of interest together.

Mr. Delacy was in Washington on business
for the law firm of which he was the junior member. The firm had discovered, in settling up an
estate, that a very valuable and expensive piece
of real estate belonged to heirs whose whereabouts
were unknown. It was in the heart of a large
city, but had been originally a Government grant
to one David Price.

There had been for many years a doubt about
the title, and the land had increased in value
until it was now worth quite a fortune.

Among the papers of this estate upon which
they had just administered, they had come across
an old paper which would clear the title if it
could be proven. It was to do this that he had
come to Washington. After proving title they
would endeavor to find rightful heirs, if possible.

His business was with the Land Office, but so
far he had met with little success.

Ralph told him that he had a friend who had
been for many years a clerk in the General Land
Office, and thought he might be able to help him.
Mr. Delacy readily consented to go with him to
call upon Jim. Mr. Donovan was well informed
on all matters pertaining to his office and advised
Delacy how to obtain the information he needed.

As day after day passed and Ralph received
no notice as to his appointment he began to get

restless and to haunt the door of the Secretary's
Office, but "he was busy," the messenger always
said.   But for the friendship with Delacy, and
the cheering talks with Jean, he would have
begun to lose hope.

He began also to worry about his finances.
What had seemed a small fortune was fast dwind-
ling away, and when that was gone there was no
more to follow.

He had been living at a first-class hotel, going
to the theatre, lunches and larks with Delacy;
also flowers and treats with Jean; no wonder his
money was going.   All this must be stopped.

Soon after he realized this fact, and that his
appointment might be still further delayed, he
hinted as much to Jean.

She suggested a boarding-house as the first
move.   So the next day found him looking out
for a "Room and Board."   This was not difficult, as nearly half the houses bear that sign in
bold, black letters in the window, or on tiny white
cards placed in some obscure corner, like people
who wish to be noticed, yet blush and stammer
when spoken to.

CHAPTER VIII

THESE little walks and talks with Jean had been such a help to Ralph, cheering his moments of depression and strengthening his higher and better nature. Listening with such sweet sympathy to all his hopes and plans, she also unconsciously restrained him in moments of temptation which had already assailed him in his idle hours.

For her he felt a friendship pure and sweet, as each day revealed the beauty of her character. But she, with the generosity of her nature in returning this friendship, gave with it the more precious gift of love.

Oh, what happy, happy days these weeks had been to her! How easy the daily task, when evening brought such pleasant company! Always gentle and kind, how her heart went out to everyone! and Dora, who had won her from the first by her great beauty, had also found a firm place in her loving heart.

Her own happiness made her more gentle with the restlessness and impatience her partner often showed.

One warm day in May, Dora had been very careless in her count, and it was only by the utmost diligence that Jean kept the work straight. Twice Dora left her seat in the midst of a package and had gone to the window, and, kneeling upon the sill, had looked out longingly.

Jean finished counting Dora's side of the work and her own, and had gone and brought her back to her seat. She laughed and said the sunshine and beauty of the day made her feel like a caged bird, and she longed to fly.

Then she would settle down and count so swiftly that Jean could hardly keep up with her, and as her fingers flew in and out the rapidly turned sheets she reminded Jean of a beautiful bird of paradise fluttering among a lot of "quaker-breasted robins."

She had not been there two months without others finding out that she was a rare bird of promise, I can assure you.

Not only those of the male sex who had been accustomed to pass through the room, had done so many times a day, but they had lingered longer at Mrs. Graham's desk, looking at Dora most of the time. Others had passed to and fro, always walking slowly as they passed Dora's end of the table. Dora seemed unconscious that she was the attraction; not so with most of the ladies in the room. Many times heads came together, and many a jest in fun or bitterness passed from one to the other about it. Some watched with eager eyes for the first glance Dora should give in return for the admiring ones cast upon her. Nearly all said that it was only a matter of time.

Jean noted all these signs; she watched them in fear and trembling. Dora had told her that she was alone in the world. This drew her nearer to Dora, and aroused in her a feeling of sisterly care; she felt she was pure and innocent, but knew also the danger of her great beauty and attractiveness. She grew firm in her resolution to protect her all she could, even though Dora had not seemed to seek her friendship.

As their positions at the end of the table exposed Dora to the full view of the gazers, Jean had gotten permission from Miss Temple to change their seats to others in the corner by the window, but the bright sunshine had absorbed more of Dora's attention than her work.

Jean had been stirred to greater efforts to win Dora's friendship by a remark she overheard while passing Mrs. Graham's desk one day after Dora had been employed about six weeks. A prominent official of the Bureau was leaning over Mrs. Graham's desk, and both were looking at Dora as they talked. As Jean passed she heard Mrs. Graham say: "Yes, she is indeed beautiful, and I will try and arrange it for you."

What could she mean, thought Jean. That she spoke of Dora she had no doubt. She felt flurried and nervous over she knew not what, as she resumed her work; that it brewed no good for Dora she felt certain. She began, with renewed ardor, to win Dora's love and confidence; but as Dora appeared to take her more into her heart, and their friendship seemed closer, she noticed that Mrs. Graham was gaining power over her also.

They were so different, Dora and Jean—with hardly a taste in common; Jean attracted and held by Dora's beauty; Dora held only by the efforts Jean put forth to hold her. Mrs. Graham, handsome, stylish, fascinating, leading a gay life—possessing the very qualities most dominant in Dora—had entered the race for control against Jean, who possessed none of these. Surely it was an unequal contest.

Dora felt unusually restless this beautiful May day, and when Jean saw her join Mrs. Graham at four o'clock, she summoned up courage to ask Miss Hart to come for a walk with her.

"I am going shopping with Mrs. Graham," Dora replied.

"Don't be afraid of your protégé, Miss Ainslie," said Mrs. Graham; "I will return her all right to-morrow"; and she gave Jean a look which told her that she read the mistrust which was plainly depicted on her face, and defied it.

Jean felt the blood mount to her face, and Dora, seeing she was hurt, came and kissed her on the cheek.

"Don't be jealous, little girl," she said, and hurried on after Mrs. Graham, who had walked on, sure that Dora would follow.

"After all, what harm can she do Dora, except cultivate her extravagance?" thought Jean. "Perhaps all my fears arise from jealousy, as Dora says."

She walked rather slower than usual down the three flights of steps out upon the west portico. At the end of Executive Avenue she met Ralph, who was waiting and watching for her, and in the pleasure of seeing him there, for he had never thus joined her before, her fears for Dora were forgotten.

Lady clerks have to shop after four o'clock, so any day between the hours of four and six you can see them hurrying from store to store in their feminine hunt for a bargain.

Pennsylvania Avenue was then the principal shopping center, as well as promenade, and it was almost entirely given over during these hours to Department clerks, male and female.

If Congress was in session you might meet a stray Member or Senator; also in the "season" a few society belles and young ladies out to see and be seen; but if you stood at Willard's and looked at the crowd passing to and fro at that time of the day it was safe to bet that five out of six were Government employes.

Of all the crowd scattering in every direction, Dora was the most observed. Never happier than when in the open air, her face took on a new brightness as she mingled with the crowd. She possessed lightness and grace of movement, and her strong vitality was never seen to better advantage than when walking. More than one turned to look as she passed.

"You are turning the heads of the gentlemen," said Mrs. Graham, noticing the attention which she attracted, and in her heart jealous of it, not liking to be overlooked.

"Am I? Well, I suppose every one can see that I am delighted to be out of office. See, here is Madame Delarue's; let us go in here for gloves."

They went in, Mrs. Graham wondering if Dora really was as unconscious of her beauty as she appeared to be.

After having completed all their purchases, and Dora having spent nearly her last cent, and inwardly wondering what she should do for the balance of the month for carfare, she turned to Mrs. Graham to say good-bye.

"I have enjoyed it so much," she said; "but I must hurry or I will be too late for dinner."

"Come home with me, Dora," said Mrs. Graham, laying her hand caressingly upon Dora's arm.

"Thanks, Mrs. Graham, but it is late now; I should be afraid to go home after dark."

"I will go home with you; or better still, you can remain all night with me. Come."

Her voice, which was always soft and low, was now very beguiling. "It is only a little way from here, and I am lonesome and want you to cheer me up."

"But you live at a hotel, and I shall not be fit to dine with you there."

"Well, we can have dinner in my room and a nice chat afterward. You know you are lonely, and I have lots of pretty things to show you, among them the new bonnet I was telling you about."

This was too much for Dora. She thought of her cheerless room, and long evening by herself, or the few "old fogies," as she called her fellow-boarders.

CHAPTER IX

DORA was delighted with Mrs. Graham's rooms. A hotel room is not usually very attractive, but Mrs. Graham had made hers beautiful by surrounding herself with luxurious couches, soft-toned draperies and bric-a-brac of taste and value—most of the latter being gifts, however.

Mrs. Graham was one of the erratic females who are to be found scattered through the Departments—women who wrap themselves in the cloak of apparent decency, and yet whose ways are questionable, who wield a strong power in and out of the Department. If they keep within certain limits, and most of them do, they enjoy all the outward respect and consideration of the most virtuous damsel. They form one of the strong elements of Washington life. They are usually women of intelligence, or beauty of face or figure; women to whom their proper places, according to a part of the life they lead, would fill them with horror and loathing. Thrown upon their own resources through one reason or another, lacking the courage to live openly up to their own moral standard, they become a female specimen of Dr. Jekyll and Mr. Hyde.

When influence alone was needed to obtain and retain a Government position, they were more numerous than under the present system of Civil

Service. Owing to that law their number is not increasing from outside, but is kept up to the maximum from within.

This is much slower, and a decided improvement over the old way of appointments. Now a woman of intelligence has a chance to enter the public service, and it remains with herself whether she comes out as she went in.

An innocent and pure-minded girl thrown daily with such women cannot help but be affected in some respects by the example they set her. Ignorance is not always innocence. The down may be brushed from the peach, yet it is still beautiful and delicious, and, although the working girl gains much undesirable knowledge in her contact with the world, she gains strength of character as well, and those who fall by the wayside are the exception.

Mrs. Graham preferred rooms in a hotel, for there her life was subject to less criticism, and the coming and going of her evening callers less noted and made gossip of than in a boarding-house.

She was a woman of little warmth of heart— one who gave little but expected much—whose passion was conquest and power.

Her mother, an embittered and deserted wife, had lived long enough to instil in her some of her own bitterness and mistrust, and to persuade her into a marriage with a man of wealth old enough to be her father. She was but sixteen when she married Mr. Graham, and the few years she lived with him had not softened her natural coldness of disposition. Soon after her marriage her mother died, and Mr. Graham lost his money in speculation. About this time she became acquainted with a prominent army officer and soon after eloped with him, leaving a little girl of two years.

Mr. Graham traced her to Washington; and, bringing the child with him, declared he would have nothing to do with either of them.

It was this child which kept her within certain limits of evil. It rather bored her; but it was still dear enough to her to make her wish to keep a good name, outwardly at least.

For the sake of appearance she obtained a position in the Treasury. When Elsie was six years old she put her in a convent school; there she had been for three years.

Mrs. Graham had not failed to note Dora's beauty, and the attention she attracted, but she took little interest in her until requested to do so by the prominent official—a man of whom she had tired and was glad to turn his attention elsewhere, having other irons in the fire, without losing her complete control over him.

She therefore began to cultivate Dora. She had also understood Jean's feelings towards her, and had been amused at the idea of such a mite setting her will against hers. She felt confident that when she was ready to use Dora she could do so.

While Mrs. Graham ordered dinner, Dora flut-

tered from one object to another, delighted with
all she saw.

"Dora," said Mrs. Graham, after the waiter
had left the room, "I know you are not comfortable in that thick dress this warm evening. Let
me give you something lighter"; and going to a
closet she took down a soft amber tea-gown.

"Take this," she said.

"Oh, Mrs. Graham, how lovely! But you are
so much stouter than I it won't fit me."

"Yes, it will; it will fit anybody. Try it."

Dora quickly put it on, and it fell in clinging
folds around her. It was made of softest Japa-
nese crêpe; such textures were rare in those days,
and this had been a gift from a friend in the
navy. It followed every curve of her lovely figure and gave the finishing touch to her marvelous
beauty.

"You only needed this," said Mrs. Graham,
tossing her a golden girdle which might have
been made for Cleopatra, "to make you look like
a goddess."

As Dora clasped the jeweled belt, bringing
the folds more closely around her, the gas lighting up the amber folds, giving a golden tint to
the dark auburn hair and a new brightness to the
yellow flashes of the eyes, she might have stood
for a Venus clothed in sunshine. Dora looked
at herself in the glass.

"The effect is not half bad," she said, laughing; "but you spoil me, Mrs. Graham, with your
beautiful rooms and dress. It will be very hard

to be Cinderella again to-morrow. And this dress," holding up the gleaming folds, "why, I should have to work for years for such a one. I don't see how I am to get even the cheapest on my salary, and I do love fine clothes."

Dora sighed, as she slowly let fall the upheld dress, pouted and threw herself with impetuous grace into a large arm-chair.

"It will remain with yourself whether you get an increase in salary or not," said Mrs. Graham, looking at Dora enviously, and noticing the abandoned grace of her position and the passionate impatience at her lot in life.

"Oh, don't, Miss Graham; that sounds so much like my old teacher. 'If you are good, study hard; you can take all the prizes,' she used to say; but I never was good, never worked hard, and never took any of the prizes, and I am sure I can never become expert in my work, as easy as it is. My mind will not stay on, 'one, two, three, four,' " she said, imitating the counting of sheets and ending in a laugh.

There was so much childish innocence with all the womanly beauty, so much guilelessness of heart with all the wilfulness of temperament, that even Mrs. Graham, cold-hearted and callous as she was, hesitated to show her her power, and while she hesitated dinner was served.

After dinner Mrs. Graham drew from her an account of her life, and how restless, unhappy and lonesome she had been the two months she had been in Washington.

CHAPTER X

"You are surprised to see me, Miss Ainslie; but I was so anxious to see you I could not wait," said Ralph, as he met Jean at the end of Executive Avenue on the day that Dora had gone shopping with Mrs. Graham.

"Have you gotten your appointment?" asked Jean, seeing that what he had to tell her was pleasant news.

"No," laughed Ralph; "not quite, but I have received a letter from the 'Judge,' and he is coming down to work for me himself. Isn't that awfully jolly of him? I always told you that he was the best friend in the world for helping a fellow. What is more, he has sent me a personal letter to one of our Senators, and I am going to hunt him up to-morrow."

"I am so glad for you," said Jean. "Failures with heroic minds are the stepping-stones to success. You have taken a good many steps, but you will succeed yet. It is, indeed, good news."

"Yes; I knew you would be pleased. That is why I came to meet you. I am going to-night with Delacy to call upon a lady friend of his who has considerable influence here among the politicians. To-morrow afternoon, you know, I go with Jim upon that long-talked-of fishing trip to

Great Falls. Delacy has concluded to go with us, so I expect we will have a jolly time. I could not keep my good news until my return, for I knew you would be glad to know that the 'Judge' was coming down."

Some of the brightness which had filled her on meeting him and which had flushed her pale face seemed to fade away at this speech.

Nearly a week before she would see him again! and she sighed.

Ralph did not notice this or her silence. He had become interested and amused at seeing six or eight little colored girls waltzing and dancing to the accompaniment of a street organ—their little, black bodies, clothed in dirty rags, swaying with natural grace and lightness, their bare or half-bare feet keeping perfect time to the waltz movement, their eyes shining, and white teeth showing as they panted for breath; but still they kept on, their faces beaming with pleasure.

Square after square had they followed that music, as the children followed the Pied Piper of Hamlin. It lured them on and on, until too dead tired to walk home.

"Where do they learn it ?" asked Ralph, as he noticed them dancing the very latest fad.

"It is born in them, I think," said Jean, as they continued their walk out Connecticut Avenue. "The children at least of that unfortunate race always seem happy. I sometimes think that Rasselas might have found his perfect happiness among them."

"That reminds me," said Ralph; "did I not see a sort of unhappy look on your face as you came up Executive Avenue? Has your beloved friend, Miss Hart, been trying your patience again?"

Jean had often spoken to him about Dora.

"Yes," said Jean, smitten with the thought that since meeting Ralph all thought of Dora had vanished.

"What has she been doing to-day to cloud your usually bright face?"

"She has been very trying all day, and this afternoon she has gone shopping with a lady."

"Gone shopping with a lady! Well, that is a grave offense!" he said, laughing. "Who would take you for such a jealous little dragon?"

"There! That is just what Dora said: 'Don't be jealous,' and then she came and kissed me," added Jean, gently.

"I don't blame her for that, I am sure."

"What nonsense!" said Jean. All the same she blushed with pleasure at the implied compliment.

"But, do you know," she added quickly, seeing he was about to continue in the same strain, "I begin to think I am becoming very meddlesome. Here I am worrying and fretting over a girl I scarcely know, wanting to restrain and advise one who is hardly a friend."

"It is your kind heart, little girl. What would I have done these two months without your friendship? Those words of Blair's are true:

'Friendship! mysterious cement of the soul; thou sweetener of life and solder of society, I owe thee much'; and I have no doubt that Miss Hart feels as grateful to you for your kind interest in her as I do—if she has made you jealous by going out with some other friend."

"Oh, you must not think I am jealous at Dora's having other friends. The lady with whom she left the office is one whose friendship I do not think desirable for any girl."

"Oh!" said Ralph, understanding more fully than she did herself the cause of her worry. "By the way, I was in hopes of seeing your friend when I joined you. I must confess you have excited my curiosity. But is not that Governor Shepherd's new home?" he continued.

"Yes, poor man; but people don't seem to give him much chance to enjoy it. If he listens to all of their complaints he must be very unhappy in his new home."

"He has a strong champion in you."

"I love my city and realize what he has done and is doing for it. You spoke about hoping to see Miss Hart. She has no friends in the city, and I am sure she would be delighted if you will go with me to call upon her some evening. Shall I ask her?"

"I have thought of asking you to do so. When shall we go?"

So talking and planning, they walked out as far as Stewart's Castle, the objective point in all Washington's strolls at that time. Standing all

alone in its then unsurpassed grandeur, it was
the herald of the magnificent buildings that have
followed, and alongside of which it soon seemed
tawdry; but in those days, like "Katisha's shoulder," people came miles to see it.

It was a lovely afternoon, and all the gay
world of fashion which was not receiving was out
calling.

The sidewalks were strewn with little bits of
white tissue paper from between visiting cards,
and crowded with the wealth and beauty of the
Capitol. They passed many a noted personage
and prominent man, foreign Ministers and diplomats of all descriptions. Although the weather
was getting very warm, the long session of Congress still kept the fashionable people at Washington.

When Jean sat alone in her room that evening
her calm, quiet face was beautiful with the love-
light of a pure soul shining softly over it. In
her simple white wrapper, and with the moon-
beams stealing in through her window garden in
little rays of holy white, touching hands and face
and hair with misty gleams of light like angels'
kisses, her beloved plants and flowers threw shadows, like the doubts and fears which fluttered
through her heart, that still was filled with pleasant thoughts, and made her look like some pure
saint etched out in black and white.

For the first time she opened the door to
hope. Never had his words and manner been
so tender. She forgot that he was elated over his

letter and at the prospect of the "Judge's" coming down. He had expressed his appreciation of their friendship, and her cheeks burned as she recalled what he had said about the kiss.

"O God!" she cried, as doubt threw a shadow over her heart, "deem me worthy of this gift, all unworthy as I am."

How happy it made her to think that she was at least sure of his friendship. Even that was sweet to her—oh, so sweet.

"Sweetener of life," he had said, and she repeated fervently, "I owe thee much."

CHAPTER XI

FROM pale moonlight and dim shadows we look into the brightly lighted parlor of Mrs. Graham, where we left Dora with her heart full of longing for fine clothes and a passionate desire for the pleasures of life excited by the possessions and insinuations of another. Clothed in borrowed splendor and her own magnificent beauty, she looked, as she felt, above the monotonous work of counting other people's money.

Mrs. Graham's conversation for the last half hour had acted on Dora like a gad-fly upon a spirited horse. It had pricked her here, bit her there, until she felt that she would almost rather do anything than continue the work she had begun for her living.

Mrs. Graham had so clothed her remarks that Dora did not know just what she meant, but was flattered into feeling above her position.

Their talk was interrupted by a gentle tap at the door. Mrs. Graham opened it and the Prominent Official stepped in.

Having been introduced to Dora, he took the chair nearest her, and the three were soon engaged in an animated conversation.

"Mark maiden innocence a prey to love-pre-

tending snares," is what might have been said by
one of experience, could they have seen the looks
the Prominent Official bestowed upon Dora.

He had thought her beautiful at the office in
her plain black dress, with the rather petulant
expression which was too often on her fair face,
with close-shut mouth and tip-tilted chin; but
to-night—the flushed face, the eyes sparkling
with excitement, the beautiful mouth softening
into tempting curves and ending in lovely dimples—dimples that were not always to be seen,
but came to view only in her happiest moment.

The rounded form, but ill-concealed in that
becoming gown, the sensuous grace of every pose,
bewitched him.

It was with an effort that he controlled himself sufficiently to keep the conversation upon
general topics. His object was not to startle her
by too sudden a show of his admiration. He
would first win her gratitude; then her.

"How do you like your work, Miss Hart?"
he said.

"I do not like work at all," Dora replied
frankly; "so I am a poor judge. As for this
work I am obliged to do, it is too monotonous to
suit me, and I am sure I can never become interested in it. You know, the mind will easily
straggle from the fingers. Still, it must be done;
but if it was not for the best little girl in the
world I fear I should have met with disgrace ere
now. She finds all my mistakes and keeps me
straight."

"There are other positions besides counting, and, you know, I am not without influence with the chief. With such a hand you ought to be a good penman. How would you like a clerkship?"

"I am not sure of my penmanship, but think such a position would be less tiresome than counting."

"And the salary so much more desirable," added Mrs. Graham.

"Oh, that would be delightful," said Dora.

"I will do my utmost to get you a good-paying promotion."

"Oh, you are very kind," said Dora, "and just when I was beginning to despair. How can I ever thank you enough if you succeed?"

"We will not talk of thanks now; it is sufficient to know I have helped you."

Dora could have hugged him on the spot, he seemed so good and kind. How was she to know that all this had been planned for just such pay?

He saw her gratitude, and a feeling of confidence in his campaign was almost about to put him off his guard, when there came a gentle tapping on the door. A look of annoyance passed over his face, and the greeting he gave to the two gentlemen who entered, though old friends, was far from cordial.

Mrs. Graham, on the contrary, greeted the elder of the two men with her sweetest smile, although she had looked a little surprised as they entered.

"Why, Senator," she said, after presenting

them to Dora, "I thought you expected an all-night session ?"

The Senator scarcely heard her, he was so intently observing Dora, who was talking to the second gentleman, whom Mrs. Graham had introduced as Mr. Lance, of ——.

Now, Mrs. Graham had begun to feel a little bored at playing the "spider and the fly," and at first felt pleased at the interruption, but on seeing this intent, admiring look upon the Senator's face, she became provoked. She by no means intended the Senator and Dora to meet. He was the card upon which she had placed her stake, and she was not yet sure of winning. She had selected this evening, thinking Congress would keep him at the other end of the city.

The cold, gray eyes looked through the long lashes. She was on the defensive now. She had no fear, however, but that she could capture this queen and put the king in check.

Meanwhile, Mr. Lance had been greatly surprised, on being introduced to this beautiful maiden, to have her come toward him so graciously and put out her hand and thank him for favors bestowed.

"You do not remember me, Mr. Lance," she said, "and yet it is to you I owe my position in the Bureau."

"Can it be possible ? Surely I have never seen you ?"

"Still, I have seen you and heard you, too, on the stump," laughed Dora, enjoying his confusion. "I went with my uncle, Reverend John Hart, of ——, to hear you speak."

"John Hart, of ——? Why, of course; how stupid of me! I remember it all now; but why have you never made yourself known to me since your arrival here?"

"I did write and thank you."

"So you did, but when I think that but for this accidental meeting I might never have known you I am tempted to scold you."

The conversation here became general, but his mind contained but two thoughts—"what was the Rev. John Hart's niece doing in Mrs. Graham's parlor? and what a glorious beauty she was!" He made up his mind to know her better.

Acting on the latter impulse, he soon found an opening to say: "Are you pleasantly fixed at the office? I might be able to help you further if you are not."

Before Dora could answer, the Prominent Official spoke up: "I have just promised to obtain a promotion for Miss Hart."

"Indeed," said Mr. Lance, and the two exchanged looks. "I begin to see," thought Mr. Lance.

"Yes," said Dora, understanding none of this by-play, "is it not kind of him?"

"Well," said the Senator, "you are playing in luck, Miss Hart, having two such influential persons interested in you. I shall not be left out in the cold, however, and you may call on me if they are not successful."

"Then," said Mrs. Graham, "we may consider Dora as already promoted, and I propose we drink to her success."

"Well said, my friend," the Senator replied.

From a little refrigerator behind a screen in the corner Mrs. Graham brought forth champagne. She did not think it advisable to have all her wines sent up from the bar.

They drank to Dora's success.

"Gentlemen," said the Senator, "I congratulate you on your protégé."

Each gentleman had a toast to propose—and Dora, what did she think of this drinking?

It seemed perfectly natural to her. She had been in the company of her mother when champagne had been drunk in honor of some success she had made, in some new opera or especially fine performance.

It simply reminded her of those times. It seemed as though the compliments and attention being paid to her now were not to herself, but to that mother, and she felt as she used to when standing by and hearing her praised.

Personally she cared little for liquor, and the same circumstances which made this scene familiar had taught her the danger of wine. She did as she had seen her mother do—take tiny sips and guard against the refilling of the glass.

Knowledge was power, and the little mouse was not to be caught with that cheese.

Again there came a tap at the door. This time it was the bell-boy, with two cards upon the tray, the other gentlemen having walked up without this ceremony. Mrs. Graham looked at the names upon the cards, thought a moment, and then gave orders for the gentlemen to be shown up.

There was safety in numbers, she thought, and the Senator's attention must be diverted from Dora.

The Prominent Official bit his lips in vexation at the frustration of all his plans for the evening, but congratulated himself upon coming early and having spoken to Dora about a promotion before Mr. Lance came in. He had the inside track, he thought, and gave the two young men who entered but a passing glance.

Not so with Dora; for the first time during the evening she felt interested.

She had felt flattered and pleased at the attention paid her, but they all seemed like old men to her, and simply amused her; but as Mr. Delacy and Ralph were introduced she felt entirely different.

Youth turns to youth as the sunflower toward the sun, and, while with the others she had been self-possessed, she felt herself blush as she met their admiring glances and had little to say.

Delacy and the Senator were old friends, and he had been several times with him to call upon Mrs. Graham. He therefore more readily entered into the general conversation, while Ralph, who felt somewhat embarrassed, contented himself with listening and looking at Dora, who sat somewhat apart from the others and was very quiet, but who caught more than one of these glances as she in turn looked toward him.

As Mrs. Graham saw the Senator cross the room and take a seat beside Dora, she proposed a game of cards. Three at least of the gentlemen present she knew to be devoted to the "festive jack-pot," and in answer to her "check" they showed their willingness to play.

They soon had a table in the middle of the room. She brought out a handsome box of chips and cards, and said:

"Who'll be banker ?"

It was an understood thing between the three elder men that whoever banked paid Mrs. Graham's losses.

They usually cut for the privilege, but strangers being present the Senator said:

"As the eldest he would take the responsibility if they promised to patronize the bank well."

Mr. Delacy was from the Southwest, and therefore knew a "thing or two" about the game; besides, he had played with the others on his former call and had carried off the laurels; it would look mean even to hesitate now. He had also found an opportunity while they were fixing the table to say to Ralph that if he was not "fixed" he would see him through.

Ralph thanked him, but said he "knew it not," and so stated when asked to join the game. He would look on and learn, he said.

When it came to placing Dora at the table the Prominent Official and Mr. Lance again ex-

changed looks. Each read the other's wish to
stake the lady should she plead poverty.

Dora declared that "she never could tell the
fathers from the sons, but she knew that a jack
and a king could not beat a pair of deuces."

"Oh, but they have, many a time," said Mr.
Delacy, and the rest said that was enough knowledge to start on.

"It is always safe to learn even from our ene-
mies," said the Prominent Official.

"Seldom safe to instruct even our friends,"
replied Dora, finishing his quotation, much to
his surprise.

Dora refused to play, just why she could not
have told. Was it because of those earnest, blue
eyes which she felt were watching her ? It must
have been, for after the others had started the
game she looked across at Ralph and felt satisfied with herself as he gave her back a smile.
For a while they sat silent observers and listened
to "I raise you," "I call you," etc., and seeing
them absorbed in the game, and receiving again a
look from Dora, Ralph quietly walked around
the table and drew a chair near her.

"I have known you by name and reputation
for some time, Miss Hart," he said.

"Indeed !" said Dora ; "how is that ?"

"Through your friend, Miss Ainslie."

"Oh, bonny Jean."

"You have a great friend and admirer in
her," he said.

"I fear I try her very much."

Seeing they were disturbing the players, Ralph proposed that they go to the other side of the room, by the open window.

This they did, and were soon in a confidential chat together, Jean's name having given them an "open sesame."

The game proved fitful and uneven; some of the players could not confine their attention to it in their usual manner, and it did not continue very long.

Dora and Mrs. Graham were soon alone, Dora having received an offer from each of the gentlemen to see her home; but on her saying she intended to remain all night, they all left together.

Outside the door the Prominent Official and the Honorable Member exchanged a few words. They were old friends, and thoroughly understood each other's ways. So when the Prominent Official told the Honorable Member to keep his hands off, that this was his affair, he laughingly consented to do so.

CHAPTER XII

THE next morning Dora and Mrs. Graham came in late together, which meant to Dora the loss of a quarter of a day's pay. She whispered to Jean that she had spent a delightful evening at Mrs. Graham's and had remained all night with her.

"I have lots to tell you when I get a chance," she said.

Jean, having also pleasant memories of her walk with Ralph, did not give as much thought to this as she would otherwise have done. But it so happened that on this morning it was almost impossible to keep one's thoughts upon any personal matter, for just over the way at the White House sweet Nellie Grant was being married. The amount of work done by the ladies, at least in the rooms overlooking the Executive Mansion, was small.

Through the open window, strains of sweet music could be heard, and they could see the very window in front of which the wedding party stood. They could see the carriages of the "favorites of fortune" as they drove up to the door. The walks were crowded with pedestrians who were interested in watching their arrival. They could tell, from the closing and pushing of this crowd, when some prominent guest arrived.

I fear that even careful little Jean passed many an imperfect sheet that day, for between her own interest and Dora, it was as much as she could do to keep the count correct. There was a great deal of talking among the counters; each had some little item to tell of the trousseau, or how they fell in love—how General Grant was opposed to the marriage. Some said the groom was immensely rich, others that he was closely connected with the throne, and nothing was uninteresting that day but their work; and although they had done less of that than usual, they were all tired out when four o'clock came.

Dora slipped her hand through Jean's arm as soon as they were down the steps, and said:

"Didn't your ears burn last night?"

"Not that I remember. Why?"

"Well, I met a friend of yours last night, and we just talked you over."

"A friend! Then I am sure my ears need not burn with shame."

"Ain't you anxious to know who it was? I've a good mind not to tell you for your not letting me know long ago that you had such a good-looking beau as Mr. Dennison."

"Mr. Dennison!" said Jean, blushing. "He is not my beau; but where did you meet him?"

"At Mrs. Graham's, last night."

"At Mrs. Graham's!" said Jean, a very queer, unpleasant feeling going through her. How could

it have happened? True, he had said he was
going to "call upon a lady," and had mentioned
no names. Neither had she when she spoke of
Dora's going out with a lady. Still, she was
not pleased at the thought of his going there.

Dora rattled on in her thoughtless way:
"Yes, and there was quite a little party"; and
she told all about her evening, not forgetting the
promised promotion.

Jean thought that, after all, she had good
cause for her doubts of the day previous.

"Are you sure," continued Dora, "there is
nothing serious between you and Mr. Dennison?
From all he said, I concluded that he was more
than a friend, he spoke so highly of you."

Jean told her how he had come into her life,
and why they had become such good friends in
so short a time.

Had Dora been a keen observer, she might have
read between the lines; but she was not.

"Well, you little blossom, I am delighted to
hear it, for I have completely lost my heart to
him. I think he is just too splendid, and if you
don't bring him around to see me I shall never
forgive you."

"We were speaking of that only yesterday";
and Jean told her of the conversation of the day
before.

Dora was delighted, and left Jean in high glee.
She had not felt so happy for many a day.

Not so Jean. She could not account for her
lack of enthusiasm in her friend's good spirits.

She who was generally so sympathetic, and had gone so far out of her way to win Dora's friendship and companionship, now that it seemed gained and their intimacy to become closer, found only a feeling of depression.

Accustomed to analyzing her emotions, she soon acknowledged to herself that it arose from a feeling of jealous fear that Dora would win Ralph from her. She felt ashamed that such a shadow should darken her love. Henceforth she would guard against such an emotion, or anything which would tend to sully the purity of that love.

Why should she set a claim to Ralph, even in her thoughts? Should he ever grow to love her, it would mean to her perfect happiness; if not, let her strive to keep and be worthy of the friendship he had given her, happy in the love she gave to him.

When Dora entered her cheerless room that night, it seemed more uninviting than ever. Neatly and plainly furnished, it contained nothing to please an artistic taste. Even its only little rocker was stiff and uncomfortable; and as Dora sat there and rocked, she could not help contrasting it with Mrs. Graham's beautiful surroundings, nor being filled with envy and discontent.

Poor Dora was like a beautiful ship, under full sail, cast adrift upon a stormy sea, without a captain to guide the way, or an anchor to hold her fast—without the memories of good home influence as a mental guide, or the proper ideas of right and wrong to keep her in the beaten path of safety.

Beautiful in every line, carrying the precious cargo of a human soul, she knew not the need of the hand at the helm—turning and shifting with every tide; now mounting a high wave in supreme delight, now plunging into the depths with a reckless disregard of all save her own sweet will; longing for the haven of her ambition, yet not knowing which way to turn to reach a port of safety—a derelict vessel, left to float alone upon the sea of a working girl's life.

If the ships cast adrift on that sea are well manned, staunch and strong, we may reasonably expect them to come safely into the harbor, better and nobler for that voyage in life. They are almost certain to meet these "derelicts," and the general advice is to give such a wide berth, and to look out only for their own safety. They see them struggling along in the stormy waters, and watch them sink deeper and deeper in the sea of destruction, when perhaps by a little effort they might have been brought safely into port.

Should it not be a part of every working girl's duty to not only keep in the right path herself, but to help guide the weaker vessels through the troubled waters of daily temptation?

CHAPTER XIII

WHEN Ralph entered Mrs. Graham's room and was introduced to Dora, his first thought was that Jean had not half told how beautiful she was. He had never imagined that any woman could be so entrancingly lovely. His next thought was that Jean was right. Mrs. Graham's influence was poisonous to her.

Although he had not said so to Jean, it was mostly out of curiosity that he had gone with Mr. Delacy to call upon Mrs. Graham, he having heard from him something concerning her; but when he saw Dora, he hardly noticed Mrs. Graham.

Many thoughts passed through his brain as he sat silently there while the others were talking. He noticed the empty wine-glasses and the flushed faces of the men, and their manner toward Dora. He hardly knew what to think. He felt instinctively that Jean would never be found in such surroundings.

He felt relieved as he noticed that she took little part in the general conversation, little thinking that it was he who had caused her silence. Then he remembered what Jean had said about her going shopping with a lady. He had

95

no doubt that she had been persuaded to remain with her.

When they asked her to join in the game, he waited with intense interest. Would she yield? When she refused, a weight seemed lifted off his mind.

It was then he caught her looking at him as if for approval, and he smiled in return. After that, reason flew, and when he had talked half an hour with her alone in the corner, had she been guilty of the vilest sin, he would not have believed it without the very strongest proof.

Longfellow says: "Talk as you will about principle, impulse is more attractive, even when it goes too far."

What Jean's sweet friendship, pure heart and upright principles had failed to win, was given without a moment's hesitation to Dora's greater charms of outward beauty.

The next day, on making inquiries about the Senator to whom he had the letter, he learned that he was ill. So full was his mind of the evening before, and of the fishing excursion, that what would have been felt as another set-back was looked upon lightly. Then he had the consoling thought that the "Judge" would be down soon to put things all right. So when he joined Jim and Delacy in the afternoon he was in a bright, happy mood. He was delighted to be out on a country road again, and when they stopped for a few moments at "Cabin John's" he grew loud in his praise of the fine bridge and lovely view, and

Jim had to almost force him back into the carriage.

Early the next morning (having stopped overnight at the only inn at the Great Falls) they were up and climbing down the steep rocks to the pools below for game fish.

Both Delacy and Ralph were enthusiastic over the beauty of the falls, and Jim was already catching fish while they were moving from rock to rock, lost in admiration over the grandeur of the scenery.

At their feet, stretching away right and left, were rugged rocks, deep purple in the shadows, lovely violet and mauve where touched by the morning sun; bold and rough and strong; piled up by the hundreds, as though to hold back the foaming waters from the falls above;—water that winds and twists, tumbles and turns, rushes and roars in a fury of watery magnificence not often equaled; now coming over a broad ledge of rock in one magnificent sweep, now fluttering down a little way off in a thin stream like a bridal veil; now bumping, jumping, bounding from ledge to ledge in a mighty haste; turning pale in anger at the rocky obstacles in the way, it gives a leap down upon some riven rock, forcing it farther and farther asunder, till, under the angry roar of the water, you hear the moan of the rocks.

The spring sunlight played upon the steeper and more precipitous banks of the Virginia side of the river, rich with luxuriant foliage, glowing with vermilion trumpet-vines and masses of laurel blooms and pink wild honeysuckle; while down the river, as far as the eye could see, is the mighty rush of the water where for miles and miles the Potomac chews, chews, and gnaws its mighty way amidst the ever-resisting rocks of what scientists say was once the coast line of the Atlantic shore. For miles the river, for miles the resisting rocks, which have grown old and scarred and wrinkled in their terrible contest with the strength and vigor of the ever-youthful water. The cuts and cliffs of the purple, defiant solid earth tell the result of the struggle against the united efforts of the little drops of water.

Down below in the water another struggle was taking place, the strong black bass buffeting that mighty current to preserve its species.

And it was to catch these game fish that this excursion had been made; so they were all soon down where the eddies swirl, interested in the sport.

Before long Jim began to get tired. It was growing very warm, and the fish harder to catch; and the contrast between his soft easy-chair at the office and standing on these sharp, hard rocks was too great for him to endure it long. So, making the excuse of going to see about luncheon, he climbed up the steep rocks, and was soon asleep under a shady tree.

In a little while Delacy ceased to fish, and seated himself on a rock not far from where Ralph stood, still interested in his line. He

braced his back against another rock and began
looking intently at Ralph; then, taking a cigar
from his pocket, he struck a light, took a few
puffs on the cigar, took it out of his mouth, looked
at the lighted end, put it back, took a few more
puffs, took off his glasses and polished them with
a fine silk handkerchief and again contemplated
Ralph.

And a fine picture of manly grace and strength
Ralph made, standing almost knee deep in the
curling, whirling water, with feet firmly braced
and body well balanced for any play the fish
might make.

His hat was pushed back from his forehead in
defiance of the sun, and the fair hair shone like
rays of gold beneath the dark brim. His cheeks
were flushed, his eyes bright with the swift, eager
light of expectation as he felt the fish nibbling
at the bright fly at the end of his rod; then a
flash of exultation as, suddenly, a stronger swirl
in the foaming current, the metallic buzzing of
the quickly turning reel, then the arching of the
light white rod, quivering with the perilous
strain, bending, relaxing as the game fish rushed
in its mad efforts to escape, now here, now there,
back and forth through the seething eddies. Oh,
what delight to watch this play! Again the slim
wand curves and strains; again the mad efforts
and wild delight; until the battle's won, and
within the net the gleaming, shining body of the
king of fishes lies, still squirming and fretting
to be free, but a captive who bravely fought for

his freedom, and who yielded only to superior skill.

Holding up the struggling fish, Ralph turned to where Delacy lay idly against the rock and exclaimed, with pardonable pride:

"A beauty !"

Delacy, who had been so silently contemplating him, removed his cigar, and, again looking at the lighted end, replied:

"For a young man born and raised in the country, you are successful in capturing beauties."

"I have been successful this morning at least, for here are four which are worthy of old Walton himself. I have always been fond of the sport and have fished a great deal, so that may account for my success."

"I am not surprised at your success in landing fish, but I must say that I was surprised at the *aplomb* with which you cornered the little beauty the other night."

"What ?" said Ralph, throwing down the fish which he had been admiring and taking a few steps nearer Delacy, his face showing the surprise he felt at the turn the conversation had taken.

"It was worthy a diplomat at the 'Court of Love.' "

"I am sure I do not understand you," said Ralph.

"Too late, Dennison, to play the innocent racket on me. I thought you inexperienced; but

for you to step in and monopolize a young lady,
as you did the other night at Mrs. Graham's,
when every man in the room—myself not ex-
cepted—was anxious to have a few minutes' private conversation with her, convinced me that
I had misjudged you.   Did you make your
date ?"

Slowly were the last words spoken; cool and
deliberate was the look accompanying them.

Ralph's face had been flushed by the heat of
the sun and the excitement of the sport, but it
was crimson now—over brow and neck a flush
of anger.

"By heavens! Delacy, I would resent your insult, but I feel you are under a terrible mistake."

"There is no need for your anger, Ralph; I
only envied you your tact and skill—your tact
in refusing the play, and your prompt with-
drawal to private skirmish.   I could see the
game was entered into by the others to avoid just
such a *contretemps.*   You surely did not miss
your opportunity, for she is certainly bewitching."

"You are under a terrible mistake, and your
surmises are a gross insult to the lady.   I know
all about her.   She is a friend of Miss Ainslie."

"How came she there, then ?   After what I
told you it certainly looks suspicious."

Ralph quickly told him all he knew of her—
all Jean had told him.   How glad he was that
he was able to clear her of all this vile suspicion!

How earnestly he labored to make it all appear to the best advantage! How valiantly he pleaded for her good name! No knight of old could more nobly have fought for his fair dame.

"Touch pitch and you become defiled"; for after exhausting all his eloquence, a faint stain still remained in Delacy's mind.

"She has struck you deeply, I see."

Again Ralph's face was crimson—this time in shame that he should have so soon betrayed his great interest in her.

Delacy laughed as he saw his confusion.

"Never mind, Ralph," he said; "I am with you. I never was so struck with a girl in my life. Is it a fair fight between us?"

At this he arose, threw away the unsmoked cigar, and they stood man to man, looking deep into each other's eyes.

"I am a true friend; I shall prove a true enemy," said Ralph.

"Let there be no enmity between us because of a woman. But, see, Jim is calling us to dinner."

They gathered up the fish and lines in silence, and in silence climbed the rocky and steep ascent; but the beauty of rugged rocks and tumbling, foaming water was forgotten.

Ralph's heart felt torn and bitter. What had he to win her with? No home, or even an income to start a home—nothing, while Delacy had rich parents and everything in his favor.

For the first time he wished he had not entered on this wild-goose chase at Washington.

Now he could not turn back; he must get a position, and then he might enter the race with Delacy—not even, he acknowledged, but still not without hope.

They were to go home the next day by the old canal, and although Ralph had looked forward to that part of their holiday as the most novel, he failed to enjoy it as he otherwise would have done.

The two friends had little to say to each other on their way home, and it might have been noticed that if one concluded to walk to the next lock, the other remained in the boat. But Jim, in his easy nature, had enough to say to the one that remained to listen.

It is needless to say that Jim never got out and walked the tow-path. It was simply pleasure to lie there at full length and be towed through the yellow water, and admire in his quiet way the many beautiful views and interesting spots as they moved slowly along by the side of the golden Potomac—past the Little Falls, the old chain bridge, which had echoed to martial footsteps not many years before; to watch the canal-boats with their little families and family wash, which somehow always seems to be going through some stage of cleanliness, and yet it and the family never seem clean.

As they neared the city, little boats with gay colors could be seen on the river, on their way with pleasure parties for the little club landings on the Virginia shore. Jim alone enjoyed the journey, and arrived home benefited by the little trip.

Soon after this Ralph and Delacy had another talk upon this subject, in which Ralph spoke plainly upon his present position.

How was it to be a fair fight when, until he received his appointment, it would be impossible for him to seriously address any one? If Delacy would make no serious move until he received that—unless it was too long delayed— then, indeed, they might start even in the fight. In the meantime they could both try to win her friendship, if not her love.

And Delacy, not to appear selfish, consented.

CHAPTER XIV

WHEN Delacy had asked for a fair fight he
was hardly sincere. He had been struck by
Dora's beauty, and seeing her in Mrs. Graham's
parlor, had drawn his own conclusions. He had
felt a little envious at Ralph's good luck at getting her all to himself, and so much had her
beauty impressed him that he had come to the
determination, while contemplating Ralph on the
rocks, that he should not keep her to himself.
He already knew the power of money in such
cases, and she was surely worth the price. On
finding he had made a mistake in his estimate of
her, and seeing that Ralph had been more seriously smitten than he had imagined, and still impressed with the strong attraction of her beauty,
he felt suddenly a more intense desire to win her
in a different way from that he had at first
intended.

He realized as he had "sized" Ralph up that
he was just the kind of a fellow a girl would be
taken with; thus his impulse to bind him over.
He quickly saw the advantage Ralph would have
through his friendship with Jean. Even after
he gave the matter further consideration, he had
no desire for a serious ending to the affair. She

would make a "stunning" companion in a flirtation, he thought. He was five years older than Ralph, and ten in experience. His father was a rich and prominent lawyer. He was an only child; he had always lived in a large city, and had experienced more than one "little affair." He was tall and good-looking, with handsome nose and mustache, but near-sighted eyes. He dressed always in the finest and best-fitting clothes, and had plenty of money to spend; had a slow and deliberate way and a self-satisfied manner, that so often belongs to those who have always had their own way from infancy.

Ralph had taken him up to Jim's, and through the latter's suggestions had found the information for which he had come to Washington. He was waiting for further instructions from his firm.

He had at first thought of a little flirtation with Jean; but he soon found out that she was unlearned in the first principles, and all the interest she had to show was given to Ralph. He now concluded he would cultivate his acquaintance with her to reach Dora.

To give him his due, he never realized that Ralph could be really in love on so short an acquaintance. He judged him entirely by himself.

In the meantime, Dora had received her promotion. She was transferred to the room where most of the clerical work of the Bureau was accomplished. She was put to work copying letters from a press copy book. She had an easy chair and nice desk. The Prominent Official had come in himself to see if her pens suited her, and if she found her work agreeable. He had stood for half an hour by her desk impressing her with the fact that if there was anything she needed to call upon him. She smiled upon him, and he was happy and left satisfied.

Jean missed her beautiful companion very much, but her duties were changed a little also. As there was no one to count with her, Miss Temple had put her in charge of the mutilated work. As the counters examined their work, they took out any defaced or torn sheets. These they exchanged for perfect ones, and it was these mutilated ones that Jean became responsible for, giving out the perfect ones and carefully counting and tying up the useless ones in packages of one thousand. The change of work was interesting to her, and Dora still sought her after four o'clock, and they walked home together each day.

The weather was pleasant and they had enjoyed many delightful walks.

A few days after the return of the fishing party, Dora and Jean had planned a little longer walk than usual out in the country, and Dora was to go home with Jean to dinner and remain all night.

The terminus of the Fourteenth street cars was then at Boundary street, at the foot of the steep hill leading up to Mount Pleasant, and Jean and

Dora were soon climbing this hill on their way
to the banks of Rock Creek.

'I know a bank whereon the wild flowers
grow," sang Jean, as they hurried through the
trees and shrubs which then lined the brow of the
hill.

"And healing waters flow," said Dora, taking
her arm and helping her over a big stump that
lay in their way.

"Undoubtedly," said Jean, somewhat out of
breath from their scramble up the hill. "Let us
rest here a moment, Dora, on this historic old
stone that marks the meridian, for the view from
this hill is one of the most beautiful of the many
around Washington; it is one of my favorite
spots."

"Is it here you find your sweet content?"

"Partly; I am a disciple of Epictetus, you
know, and he teaches: 'Seek not that the things
which happen should happen as you wish, but
wish the things which happen to be as they are.'
Then, you may not think it, but I am an actress."

"You an actress!" and Dora's laugh echoed
over the hills, attuned to the melody of the birds.

"Yes; I play a part each day. The rôle assigned me is that of a Government 'countess,' and
it is a title of which I am proud, because it makes
me a minute part of the running gear of the
great Republic of the United States. If I could
have chosen my rôle in life, it would have been
the home and little ones, but the Master has de-

creed otherwise, so I aim to play the part assigned me naturally and faithfully."

"Oh, but, Jean, it is so monotonous!"

"Not at all, if you allow your imagination to help you. I say to myself in the morning: 'I must go to *my* Treasury and count out *my* money to send out into the world.' I play the part of a generous 'countess,' with millions to give away, and I see to it that each and every sheet of money that passes my hands is perfect, free from blemish, as all that pertains to Government work should be. In working for the Government I am really working for myself as an individual part of that Government."

Seeing that Dora looked very serious, she quickly added, to prevent further discussion on the subject:

"See! that was the scarlet flash of the tanager, and there goes a gorgeous yellow oriole."

"Oh!" said Dora, jumping up. "I have never seen the oriole."

"It has flown to that tree across the field; let us see if we can find its nest."

"Let us run," said Dora; and like two children out from school, they ran across the field of daisies that crowns the hills that bound the picturesque creek.

The shadows of night were near before they returned home, and Mrs. Donovan's dainty repast was somewhat spoiled by the delay.

Dora was delighted with Jean's cosy room, and complained of her cheerless and unpleasant lodging. This gave Jean the opportunity to make a proposal, upon which she had been meditating ever since Dora's promotion.

"Mrs. Donovan has the adjoining room vacant. How would you like to have it?"

She knew Mrs. Donovan would be pleased to let it, for she had said as much a few days previous.

"That would be delightful," said Dora.

"It is not as pleasant in the daytime as this, as the backyards of Washington are terribly neglected, but we could have the door open between the rooms, and I would share this with you as much as possible."

Dora clasped her around the waist and kissed her impulsively.

"You are certainly the dearest little thing in the world, and I have been so lonely and unhappy, and would have been more so but for you. Let us go down and see Mrs. Donovan about it at once."

Mrs. Donovan was glad of this opportunity to please Jean, and also to add to her income.

Dora was delighted, and showed her pleasure in her bright, happy manner.

She was soon at home, filling the parlor vases with the daisies they had gathered, when Mr. Delacy and Ralph were ushered in.

In her simple white dress, and field flowers in her hands and pinned on her bosom and in her hair, she looked purer and lovelier than ever.

Both the young men felt the change. It was

like turning from passion to love. The slight embarrassment which she had felt on their approach before was not visible now. She was her bright, winning self again.

As she came forward to greet the young men, still holding the bunch of daisies in her hand, she looked the embodiment of "Spring." No wonder that Jean, with her sweet, pure face and gentle, unassuming manner, was overshadowed by her companion's bright beauty and ready wit. But Jean never thought of this. The evening was perfectly delightful to her. She felt a sort of pride in Dora's success, as one who discovers a bright jewel and holds it up for admiration delights in the sparkling light, and the applause of the beholder. Dora divided her smiles equally between her two admirers.

Ralph felt the embarrassment of his position more than Delacy did, and therefore showed to the least advantage. Once, however, he gained a smile, a look that filled him full of hope.

Dora's nervous hands had been playing with the daisies which she had kept upon her lap. A little "nun demure," as Wordsworth calls the daisy, fell from her lap to the floor. Delacy stooped and picked it up, and throwing away a fine moss-rose bud he wore in his coat, put the daisy in its place.

"How can you so cruelly throw away one flower for another? This is still fresh and beautiful," said Dora, taking up the discarded rose.

"All flowers must hereafter give way to the

daisy from to-night," he replied, a meaning look accompanying the slow, soft words.

"But to me the rose must remain the queen," and Dora stuck the rose within her belt.

"Mr. Dennison," she said, "is now the only one without Nature's favorite flower. Are you as fickle as your friend?" she continued, as she handed him a daisy.

"You see," pointing to his empty button-hole, "I wear no other colors."

It was then she gave him the smile, the glance that filled him full of joy and kindled the fire of hope.

"I think," said Jean, going to the piano, "as we have been among the daisies all the evening, you might sing this for us," holding up a song then very popular, "The Beautiful Daisies."

"That is very sad, dear; but I will sing it if you wish."

"And as we gather around you, each wearing the snowy blossoms, we will call ourselves the 'daisy chain,' " said Delacy.

Dora's wonderfully sweet voice had been finely cultivated; she had studied for years with the prospect of going upon the stage, where she would have been a great success.

She would never have thought of selecting this song, although then very popular, as her taste had been cultivated as well as her voice; but Jean had asked it. It proved rather depressing; but this was overcome by their surprise and admiration for her beautiful voice.

Even lazy Jim had gotten up from the lounge in the adjoining room to come and listen. Marie had also dropped her sewing and joined the little group in the parlor. All had some words of praise to bestow upon the fair singer, and asked for more.

"After so many compliments, I shall have to do myself credit," she said, and sang an operatic aria with great dramatic power and expression.

Song followed song until it was quite late before the two young men took their leave, each more captivated than ever.

Before they left they invited Dora and Jean to go to hear the "Marine Band" in their weekly concert at the "White Lot" the following Saturday.

Saturday afternoon proved a charming one, and Dora, in her simple white dress and big leghorn hat, looked like a young princess in her palace garden, surrounded by her court. Nor was the castle wanting, for the White House overlooked the lovely scene. The crowd was not quite the same as can still be found there each Saturday during the months from May to October. Then it was quite the style for the most exclusive to be seen there at the concert on the green lawn of the President's mansion. Now too many "dusky beauties" are apt to avail themselves of this privilege.

This was the beginning of the intimacy between the four young people. One pleasure followed close upon another. Drives to the Soldiers' Home, moonlight excursions down the river—in fact, all the pleasures of the place and season for those not in the political or "society" circles of Washington life.

Dora was amused, therefore she was happy. The long day at her desk did not seem half so tiresome now that she had some pleasure to look forward to of an evening, or some pleasant recollection of the previous evening to commence the day with. She smiled first upon one young man and then the other. There is no use denying that she took delight in raising the hopes of both; but no sooner did the hopeful one seem to claim a preference, than she turned with her sweetest smile to the other. Not only was she naturally a coquette, but she was really for some time uncertain as to which she did prefer.

Ralph's lack of funds kept him back many times, and although she did not understand this, his seeming diffidence often piqued her into bestowing her favors upon his rival.

Many a miserable night did Ralph spend through this awful lack of money. It was Delacy who hired the teams, and planned the trips, who attended to all the details, and extended the invitations. He was very nice about such things, and always included Ralph and Jean in these invitations in a manner that Ralph could not refuse without seeming boorish. This threw Ralph and Jean more together, and Jean was therefore happy, and never a suspicion of the true state of affairs crossed her mind.

She always took things as she found them, making the best of them when unpleasant, and enjoying these new pleasures with sweet contentment, never looking underneath the rose to find the thorn.

Ralph, however, was far from happy. His pride suffered, as he was forced by necessity to stand aside and let Delacy pay so often for their evening's pleasure. In a little while this became more than he could stand. He could not have endured it as long as he had but for Dora's sweet smile and winning ways when she felt kindly toward him; but just as soon as he felt that he was gaining ground with her, Delacy would step in with some plan for an outing that would give him the right to monopolize Dora's society.

At last Ralph decided that he would not be beholden to Delacy in this matter, so concluded, as he could not very well refuse the invitations (which were generally given before the others), to remain away for a while. This, indeed, was almost a necessity, so low were his funds. He had already written home once for money, and he knew they could not very well spare him more. So for over a week his friends saw nothing of him.

CHAPTER XV

Dᴜʀɪɴɢ that time he wrestled with the demon despondency. Rivalry had taken the place of friendship, and comradeship with Delacy was no longer a solace, nor could he turn to Jim's cosy parlor with the old freedom since Dora had become an inmate there.

No official document was received in any mail. The mere sight of the Secretary's door had grown hateful to him. His love was his despair.

Until he met Dora he had never lost hope; it had varied, but it still left him cheerful and happy, and in a measure patient to wait his turn.

Now each day, each minute, proved almost unbearable. Congress, he was afraid, would soon adjourn, and with it his last chance, if the "Judge" failed to arrive in time to get the indorsements he had mentioned in his letter. He had already been detained by some law business in the village.

Ralph had tried in vain to get another interview with the Honorable Member, but there was always some excuse; he had written, but in reply the Honorable Sir had said it remained entirely with the Secretary. Ralph was a witness to what he had said. He advised Ralph to have patience until the Secretary had time to attend to his case.

At the Secretary's door he had always met with the same reply: "The Secretary is busy, but you can leave your card," which, of course, the Secretary never saw.

The messenger knew his business too well to bother the Secretary with the card of an applicant who he could plainly see was without influence.

His money was nearly gone, which, after all, was the root of the evil. If he only had a little more, he could still afford to wait.

The thought of leaving Washington now nearly drove him to despair.

He moved into a cheaper boarding-house in a less desirable neighborhood, took a small hall room in the third story, and nearly died with the heat and the poor sanitary condition of the house. His clothes were far too heavy for the climate, and he longed for his cool mountain air.

He also began to take his meals at the cheap restaurants, so as to save the money to keep his linen in good form and to otherwise brighten up his personal appearance. He could not bear to look shabby; fortunately, he was one of the few men whose clothes seemed to retain their good shape. His coat never "hitched up" in the back, and he nightly wrestled with the slightest tendency of his trousers to bag at the knees. He was not vain, but neat, so he willingly denied his appetite to pay his laundry bill.

The days were hot and dreary, the nights long and sleepless, till the coming of the "Judge."

No wonder that, when, in answer to his telegram, Ralph met him at the depot, he exclaimed: "Why, Ralph, boy, have you been ill?"

"No," said Ralph; "but this weather is trying to me. This has been my first experience with warm weather in the city, you know."

"Yes, and of other things besides," the "Judge" replied, seeing not only the loss of the flush of youth, which had fled never to return, but the signs that anxious watching and waiting leave upon the youngest face. "We'll fix you all right, however, in a few days."

"How can I ever thank you for all the trouble I am giving you? I feel it is a shame to bring you 'way down here in this hot weather."

"You know, I have other business beside yours; I want to see about a pension for Mrs. Lockley. I mean to kill two birds with one stone," he said, laughing.

"Nevertheless, I shall never forget this, nor all the many kind things you have done for me."

"That's all right, boy; let's see about dinner."

Ralph spent the evening with him at the hotel, and they had much to say to each other.

The first thing the "Judge" did next day was to hunt up the Honorable Sir. Ralph told him that Congress was in session night and day, and he would have to try his luck in seeing him at the Capitol.

"Do you think he will see you?" asked Ralph.

"See me? You can just bet he will, and hear me, too. Why, boy, I put that man where he is now; I not only got him his first lift, but, without my help, he would have been left on his election; and what is more, he wants to come down here again, and he knows if he turns me down now, he will pay for it next fall"; and with the energy of a younger man he started for the Capitol, and, as Ralph did on his first appearance, there sent in his card. But unlike Ralph's reception, the Honorable Sir returned in person, and greeted him with effusion, and in a few minutes they were comfortably seated in the "lobby" —that mysterious realm where, if the walls had mouths, as walls are said to have ears, the country would resound with wondrous tales of the undertow of politics.

The Honorable Sir began by trying to impress him with the fact that he was very busy and that his vote was absolutely needed in a very few moments. But the "Judge" was not to be "bluffed." He told them that he had come down to find out why he had not had Ralph appointed.

"Why, my dear friend, do you think that I run the Departments? I took the young man personally to see the Secretary, and he promised to find a place for him."

"Well, he has been a pretty long time about it, so I have come down to have you go up with me to jog his memory."

"Why, 'Judge,' you cannot expect me to hound a man in his position? My pride, however, for-

bids me asking the same favor of a man twice";
and he puffed with an air of importance.

"This is the first favor I have asked you, after
the many I have done you. Put your pride in
your pocket, as I did for you at the last election.
Did I hesitate then?"—and I fear the good old
"Judge" swore as he grew red with anger—
"Damn me, man, where will my pride be next
fall?"

The Honorable Sir was in a pickle; beads of
perspiration decked his brow.

Why had he been such an ass as to go back to
the Secretary on taking Ralph there, he asked
himself now.

He had misjudged his man, and he could never
face him now, even if the Secretary would receive him, which he had refused to do ever since
that event.

His reason for doing Ralph such a mean turn
had been because he had intended asking the Secretary, in a few days, for the appointment of a
"person in whom he was interested," and did not
care to have Ralph's appointment counted against
him. As he had been "turned down" by the Secretary, he had sought his favor elsewhere; now
he must get out of this scrape as best he could
and please the "Judge," too, if possible.

"Let me assure you, 'Judge,' that I want to
please you in this matter, but the truth is that
certain things have transpired since then between
the Secretary and myself, and I would only do

your friend harm by going to the Secretary about him."

"Are you trying to squirm out of this?" asked the "Judge," giving him a searching look. "I don't intend to be trifled with in this matter."

"On my word, I am not, and to prove it, I tell you what I will do. It is what I have never done," he boldly asserted; "I will sell my vote for it."

Seeing the "Judge" look puzzled, he continued:

"I will get you the endorsements of the whole delegation of the State and a few of the most prominent members besides. The vote on the question pending will be very close—so close that one or two names may decide it. I have it, for reasons I need not explain, in my power to throw it either way. Their endorsements to your friend's papers will be given very willingly, I assure you, and they will be strong enough to get him into any of the Departments here. Will this satisfy you?"

"Yes, if they prove successful."

"No doubt of that. I had better set about it at once, for time is precious."

"When can I have them?"

"To-morrow afternoon."

"Very well. Shall I come here for them?"

"Yes; it will be best, if not too much trouble."

"Nothing is a trouble to me when working for a friend," replied the "Judge."

CHAPTER XVI

RALPH was delighted when he heard the good news. His imagination ran riot of all the things he would do when he got his appointment. He almost ran the poor, tired "Judge" up to Jim's that evening.

Of course, the "Judge" was anxious to see Jim, but "why such a rush?" he at last exclaimed, out of breath.

Ralph laughed and said his feet had wings tonight, and begged forgiveness for his thoughtlessness. They were all glad to see the "Judge" at Jim's, and when he told what he had accomplished in Ralph's case, all were certain that Ralph's worries would soon be over.

Dora had been very happy in fixing up her room at Mrs. Donovan's. The room had been unfurnished, and Mrs. Donovan had allowed the girls to furnish it to suit their tastes, so that they kept within the amount she felt she could afford. Dora made many plans as to what she would do, "just as soon as she was paid off," and was more delighted than ever over her increase in salary, and in consequence was unusually pleasant to the Prominent Official as he made his daily call at her desk.

He was a little put out at her changing her residence, as it interfered with many of his plans. He told her she was making a mistake in connecting herself so intimately with people who would never be a help to her. She said they were kind, true friends, and that was all she asked of them, and as such they gave the greatest help she then needed. He was careful not to offend her, so bided his time. He was also somewhat provoked at the way Mrs. Graham had acted in positively refusing to get Dora to her room again until Congress had adjourned and the Senator away, as he likewise had seemed anxious to cultivate his acquaintance with her. So the Prominent Official had been obliged to wait.

Mrs. Graham had still continued her apparent friendship, and had in a number of little things done and said kept Dora interested in her.

She had also advised Dora not to take up her residence with Jean, but to take a small room in the hotel with her. She could get her board at reduced rates, she told her, and although Dora rather liked the idea of a hotel life, this offer came too late, as she had already accepted Jean's proposal.

Both Dora and Jean noticed Ralph's absence, and Jean had been made unhappy over it, as she feared he must be ill. She spoke to Jim about this when a whole week passed and they heard nothing from him.

He would hunt him up, he said; but as the next day proved very warm, he hastened home, and when she inquired again about him, Jim said he would go to-morrow.

The truth was that Jim could not bear to do anything after leaving the routine work of his desk, at any time, and during the warm weather any effort out of the usual run seemed almost impossible.

To add to Jean's worry, Delacy, who missed no opportunity of calling, told them that Ralph had moved, and he had not seen him since the last evening they had spent together there; neither had he sent or left his address.

Jean's heart was sick with fear and anxiety, which she had to keep to herself, as pride bade her guard her secret.

These visits of Delacy's were trying times to her, but Dora seemed to enjoy them very much, as he endeavored to interest and entertain her, and always had something new in the way of pleasures to propose. Dora sang song after song, while poor little Jean sat silently by worrying over the absent one; so when Ralph came in with the "Judge," looking so happy, but worn and tired, she alone noticed the change that had come over his face.

He had been ill, she felt sure; but as Jim, in his careless way, told him Jean had nearly sent him out to hunt him up in the hospitals, as she thought he must be sick, he answered, "No," but that he had suffered from the heat.

He did not look at her, and she felt this change in his manner, and missed the bright, responsive smile, the old cordial looking to her for sympathy, to which she had grown accustomed and which had become so dear.

He hardly looked at her as the "Judge" told of his success. It would not have been thus a few weeks previous.

She was certain, although he had denied it, that he was not well, and she longed to do something to bring back the old look again. Never once did she associate Dora with the cause of this change, although she saw him looking long and intently towards her; but his manner towards her was rather distant, and his words few, because, from the fullness of his heart, he could not speak as he wished.

Dora did not understand Ralph's manner towards herself. He had pleased her fancy on their first acquaintance. Why he had grown indifferent towards her, as his avoidance seemed to indicate, she could not tell.

She would not waste any more thoughts on him; his friend was more appreciative, however, she thought, as she recalled some of his softly whispered words.

The next morning the "Judge" spent in attending to the pension, and Ralph passed another long and restless day, and when the "Judge" in the evening handed him the long list of endorsements, he was hardly as enthusiastic as he should have been. "Hope deferred maketh the heart sick," and he was really half sick in body and mind.

The next morning the "Judge" started out early to see the Secretary.

Ralph was afraid the "Judge" would not be admitted, he having been refused so many times by the black guardian of the formidable door; but the "Judge" had no such timidity. He told Ralph to wait in the hall for him, and marched up to the messenger in his most pompous and majestic manner.

Had he been judge of the Supreme Court he could not have assumed greater dignity of bearing, or commanded more profound attention from the messenger, who took him at once for some such high official, as he asked, not meekly as Ralph would have done, but in a tone of one in authority, "Is the Secretary busy?" as though, of course, there was no question of his being admitted under ordinary circumstances, and in a few moments he was calmly talking to that person in the most friendly manner.

The Secretary had received him politely and read the long list of names. He also recalled the interview with the Honorable Member, but did not mention the latter to the "Judge."

It had been his intention to appoint Ralph at the time, for he was disgusted with the underhand way of the Member; but it had slipped his memory. He rang a bell (in these days he would have touched a button) and a messenger came. He sent him for the rest of Ralph's papers, which had been neatly folded, nicely briefed and catalogued, and put on file in the appointment division from which they were now resurrected.

The Secretary put them all together, after looking them over, and marked them "special" in blue pencil, and then told the "Judge" that Ralph's appointment would be sent to him in a few days, if he would leave his address.

Ralph meanwhile had been walking up and down the hall, and when he saw the "Judge" come out smiling he knew that all was well. He was so unnerved and unstrung by his long waiting that if he had not taken the "Judge" up to some cases of curious old models of patents, and thus given himself time to recover his composure while the "Judge's" attention was diverted elsewhere, he felt he would be betrayed into showing his weakness.

The "Judge" was very much interested in those old relics, showing, as many of them do, the crude form of the first inventions of many now almost perfect machines. He wandered from case to case, Ralph patiently following, thinking of the many times he had walked around them in his despondent moods, after having been refused admittance to the Secretary.

The next day the "Judge" and Ralph went up to the White House, for the "Judge" declared he could not leave the city without seeing the great "General"; so they wandered through the different rooms and through the long conservatory, they peeped into the State Dining-room and walked the full length of the East Room, and looked out on the green lawn and river beyond, and regretted that the monument was still unfinished.

At last the great man appeared, and took them by the hand. One of the Nation's greatest heroes stood before them, and all else was forgotten.

In a few days Ralph received his appointment as "Special Agent" in the General Land Office, and was to report for duty the following Monday.

CHAPTER XVII

ONCE more Hope threw her mystic mantle over Ralph. All the disappointments of the past were forgotten; hope deferred, alarms of love, doubts and fears, all were hidden from his view. The scintillating rays of those magic folds could reflect only the most beautiful thoughts of the future. The past worries, for the time at least, were already dim shadows. He forgot that he had suffered even to the pangs of hunger, that his overcoat and winter clothes were still at the pawn shop. He remembered only that he might now woo Dora. All day long, in his little narrow hall room under the roof, he sat and dreamed of what this wooing meant to him. The check he had been obliged to put upon his love had but added strength to his passion. Would the long, hot, sultry day never end? was his one impatient thought. He longed for night, that he might hasten to his beloved, and begin the wooing of the "Queen of Girls."

It was raining very hard when night, in its due time, drew near. Nature was seeking her own relief from the sultry heat of the last few days. The wind blew the young trees, so newly set in rows, as though it wished to mar the symmetry so nicely planned by man. The lightning flashed as though to show the wind which ones to strike, and the thunder roared as if in glee to see them bend and snap their tender stems, and yield up their fresh young lives, or turn and twist until they were deformed forever; and so we see them to-day, old trees, but still showing the effect of that cruel summer storm of their youth—the weak ones fallen, the unfortunate ones deformed for life; while the same storm brought renewed vigor to others, which the dry, hot weather had so nearly laid low.

And so it is with life. We stand together side by side. Over us all the same storm passes, and yet how different the effect! Is it that one is weaker than the other, or does some great unseen power flash the light that only the right one may fall by the way? giving life to one, at least a living death to the other, who can tell?

But the storm had no power to keep Ralph indoors. He slipped quickly along, darting across the falling branches, and jumping lightly over the streams and ponds made by the remodelling and paving going on in nearly every street. Sometimes he would have to wait for a flash of lightning to guide his way, for, as the city had a contract with the moon, there was no gas lighted. The lamp-lighter was slow in getting around in a storm, when, according to the calendar, there should be bright moonlight. Such rash extravagance, even in those days, as gaslight and moonlight was not to be thought of in Washington.

Any little town could put it to shame in that respect with its electric lights.

But what cared Ralph for the storm, except as it delayed his footsteps? The joyous light of youthful anticipation had returned. The quick, buoyant step was as light as on the first night of his call at Jim's. Once again it was Jean who let him into the brightly lighted hall.

As she looked at his bright face and saw the old animated look she had so missed from it, she guessed immediately his good news.

"You have been appointed," she said as he was still busy shaking the rain-drops from his hat and clothes, as the umbrella had been useless most of time owing to the wind.

"Yes," he said; "how did you know?" As he spoke he was looking over her shoulder into the room beyond, where he could see Dora standing under the bright gaslight.

"I read it in your face," Jean answered softly. But Dora had smiled, and he heard her not; and as she turned to hide the tears of joy in her tender, loving eyes, he passed quickly into the room and left her there with her heart beating wildly in her rejoicing at his happiness, and without the slightest suspicion that it was aught but delight at his appointment that she saw in his face. She would no longer have been ignorant of the true state of affairs had she seen that face as he hastened toward Dora with outstretched hands. He seemed about to clasp her in his arms; indeed, it was only with a strong effort that he refrained from doing so.

As Dora met that look she was startled out of her usual self-command. She blushed; and as he still held her hands, which she unconsciously had placed in his, an emotion passed through her she could never forget. It seemed impossible for Ralph to speak, and she for once knew not what to do.

"Isn't the good news delightful! The long-looked-for appointment come at last!" said Jean, coming into the room; and, seeing them standing hand in hand, supposed that Dora was congratulating him upon his appointment. Without waiting for an answer, she passed on to the room beyond to tell the "good news" to Jim and Marie.

Dora withdrew her hands with a more vivid blush, and turning her back to hide her embarrassment, she walked over to the piano. What a fool, she thought, she had made of herself; thinking that it was love for herself she had seen in his face, when it was only his pleasure over his appointment!

A fierce anger at herself took possession of her which made Ralph's wooing a stormy sea for many a day to come. Her pride was strong and her temper wilful, and her impetuous disposition spared herself least of all.

Ralph was too busy trying to recover his own equanimity to notice her embarrassment, and so when Jim and Marie came in to express their delight he was glad at first at the interruption, but as they all remained in the room during the whole of his call he had time to regret it.

Jim had so much to say about the work Ralph would have to do that he became quite energetic in giving his good advice. At last, having talked them all tired, he declared they ought to celebrate it in some way, and many plans were talked of; at last it was decided that they would take a holiday the next day and go down to Mount Vernon.

The tomb of the "Father of his Country" was the proper place, Jim said, for Ralph to lay his thank-offering upon for being permitted to "slave for this great and glorious Republic."

Seeing there was no chance of a few words alone with Dora that night, Ralph took his leave with a heart full of hopes of the opportunities the day's outing might bring forth. The only unpleasant thought about this was that he was to see Delacy or leave a note at his hotel that night on his way home, inviting him to go with them. Although the thought of Delacy's making one of the party was unpleasant to him, he still felt that it was just. He had pledged for a fair fight, and it was well that Delacy should know that he had received his appointment and was ready to take an active part in the fight for Dora's love. He realized how near he had come that night to betraying his love, and how difficult it would be to keep silent on the morrow should an opportunity present itself. He was willing to do what he thought was right, especially as he knew Delacy had waited so patiently for him to receive his appointment before declaring his love to Dora.

On reaching the hotel he was much surprised to learn that Delacy had left that evening for home.

The next morning he received a letter in the early mail explaining this sudden departure. Delacy's mother was very ill, and his father had telegraphed for his immediate return. There were words in that letter which changed all Ralph's bright anticipations for the day (even with Delacy a part of it) to bitterness.

"You will remember our agreement," he wrote, "that it is to be a fair fight. I have waited at your request until you should receive your appointment; now I ask you, should you receive that appointment during my absence, to wait until my return before pleading your suit. I rely upon your honor not to take an undue advantage of my absence. I will return as soon as possible; but should it prove longer than I hope, (for I trust to find my dear mother better), I will write and we will come to some decision in the matter."

It did not need a second reading for Ralph to realize that here was another check to his fond hopes—another obstacle to his love-making.

He would have need of strength, great strength, he told himself, to pass through this with honor, and what if, by all this delay, he should lose her? The thought was madness. He had not much time to think, however; he must be at the boat to meet them, and he must be true to himself; but all the glory had gone from the day.

This telegram calling him home had caused Delacy to sit down and think seriously of his feelings toward Dora.

We have seen his state of mind when he asked for a fair fight. Had he become more serious as he had seen more of Dora, and found her not only more beautiful, but become firmly convinced of the wrong he did her in his first estimation of her?

This was the question he asked himself as he felt obliged to leave an open field to Ralph. He had to confess that his feelings toward her had grown deeper than he ever expected them to, and that to give her up now would be almost impossible, especially as he knew Ralph was only waiting for the opportunity to win her himself. She was so entrancingly lovely that to possess her, he thought, would almost make up for all he would lose by marrying her and settling down. There was the rub. It was the horror or dread of marriage ties as to himself that he felt made him hesitate the most. It was a mistake for a man so young in life to tie himself down to one woman. He did not feel half through "sowing his wild oats," and he would wish to remain true to the woman he married; and what if in time he should tire even of Dora?

And then, even though he were perfectly satisfied with Dora, and willing to marry her, how would the match be regarded by his parents? He had not any doubt about this. His lady mother would shrink from a working girl, however charming, and one whose mother had been an actress would be still harder to accept. His father had made money his idol, and upon that point Dora would surely not be an acquisition.

He had always had his way, and although he dreaded the opposition that he knew they would make, it was not the real cause of his hesitancy. It was simply his dread of the change marriage would make in his daily life, and the feeling that he would not come up to the test of such a life.

Still, there was Dora, and there was Ralph waiting for her. He would not yield her up to him; he could not give her up. He had no doubt as to whether she would accept him. She had shown her preference for him so often, he thought, that he had the best chance of winning her.

As he must leave her, and not knowing of Ralph's appointment and thus the release of his promise, he concluded to bind him over until his return, especially as he would not have a chance of seeing her before his departure.

He was not entirely sorry for this. The present state of his feelings warned him that if she seemed saddened by the idea of this parting, he could not remain silent. It was well that he would have a week or two to think about the matter of marriage. "A thing so easily gotten into, so hard to get out of," he said to himself.

Nevertheless, he wrote her a sweet little note, which he sent to the office, telling of his great sorrow at being obliged to leave the city without seeing her, etc., and he bound Ralph by his honor not to speak to her of love.

CHAPTER XVIII

THE sun rose in all its crimson splendor after the storm, which had lasted all night, and the lovely city looked bright and smiling after its bath, with its green parks and sparkling trees more beautiful than ever.

But the loveliest thing in that whole city was Dora's face, as she looked out of the window to greet the morning sun.

Her delight at finding that it had cleared, and they were to have a lovely day for their excursion, made her forget the poor opinion which she had of herself when she went to bed, for having, as she feared, betrayed the emotion she felt on meeting that passionate look of intense love on Ralph's face, which she afterward attributed to personal delight over his appointment.

A whole day of pleasure, was her first thought. A whole day out in the open air, away from pen, ink and paper.

Then she remembered her anger at herself on the night before, and she was glad that she would so soon have an opportunity to convince Ralph that if she cared for any one person in the world it was his friend, Delacy.

The anticipations for the day were delightful.

From the depression of the night before her spirit rose like a bird at the break of day, and she sang like one while making her toilette, taking particular pains to choose a becoming one.

"Oh, Dora!" at last said Jean from her room, where, already dressed, she was giving her two pet birds their breakfast, and who were trying their best to outsing Dora. "Between you and the birds the neighbors will lose their morning naps and baby Jean be awakened before her time, and therefore tired before the morning is half over."

"Jean," said Dora, coming to the door, which always stood open between the rooms, "how can you be so placid going around among your flowers and birds, just as though nothing was going to happen, and we to have a holiday? As for me, I am giddy. Expectation whirls me round. The imaginary relish is so sweet that it enchants my sense. As I have not much of the latter quality, you will have your hands full to-day to keep me in check."

"Am I always to rectify your mistakes, Dora?" said Jean.

"If you undertake that, the burden will be greater than you can bear. I am like that 'Sweet Love,' that Spenser tells of, 'that doth his golden wings embay in blessed nectar, and pure pleasure's well,' and to-day I shall probably sink in over my head. But you shall be my life-preserver. When I look upon you I shall not drown."

"Dora, you do talk so wildly. I am sure I don't want to be a check upon your pleasure."

"Really?" laughed Dora. "Well, you are." Seeing that Jean looked puzzled, and not wishing further questioning, she said: "I wish I were more like you, little blossom," holding Jean's face between her hands. "But, however much I may try you, remember I appreciate your kindness to me," and she stooped and kissed her.

Jean's face was sunshine once more, as Dora passed out of the room, telling her to hurry up.

Jean had also arisen in high spirits, and with a blithe joy in her heart, and to her the day seemed full of promised sweetness. How could she tell they were the "fleeting joys of Paradise dear bought with lasting woes?"

All were disappointed when Ralph met them at the boat alone and told of Delacy's sudden departure.

Dora was disappointed, and she felt it her duty to impress upon Ralph how terribly sorry she was; and as he saw how this disappointment affected her, he felt tempted to jump overboard, but instead turned his attention to Jean and the others, and they were all soon aboard the gay little steamer "Arrowsmith," which then made the trip to the historic and sacred spot of Mount Vernon, where lie the remains of our great and glorious Washington.

Situated on the hill of green with the broad river at its feet, it retains much of its old-time

appearance, and there are gathered the relics of
George and his beloved Martha, and within those
walls the home life of that illustrious family is
made very clear to those who wander from room
to room.

It was a perfect day for a trip down the river,
made delightfully fresh and cool by the storm of
the previous night, and our little party had been
very merry and apparently happy on their way
down the Potomac—past the green trees of the
Arsenal and old historic Geesborough, the ancient town of Alexandria, where every foot of
ground is a leaf out of the ancient history of
America.

Before reaching Mount Vernon they decided
to have lunch upon the boat, that the time spent
at the old homestead might be given to sightseeing
and enjoyment. Soon the smiling captain had
them supplied with a table, and even went so far
as to lend them a can-opener, despite the fact that
nine out of ten upon whom he conferred this
favor forgot to return the article.

When they reached Mount Vernon they were
all ready to lay a very joyous homage upon the
sacred tomb, which mark of respect in those days
was very likely to be bestowed upon the icehouse
by mistake.

Dora still retained her high spirits, having recovered from her first disappointment over Delacy's absence. She found many ways to torment
Ralph, and yet have a gay time herself. Ralph,
like the proverbial swain, was fain to follow at

the slightest sign. He left no effort untried to make her comfortable and her day pleasant, only too happy that she had not remained in silent grief over the absent one.

The old hill at the landing was much more steep, and harder to climb, than the present one; but Ralph and Dora started off briskly, leaving the others far behind in a little time.

Baby Jean cried for flowers by the wayside, and Jean lingered behind with her to gratify her wish. The others were nearly all up the hill ere she, with her little charge, had made half the ascent. Then baby Jean grew tired and asked to be carried, and Jean took her in her arms and slowly continued up the hill. The rest stood at the top, enjoying the lovely view.

At last Ralph turned and saw her. With a few rapid strides he was by her side, and had taken the baby from her.

"Why did you not call me?" he said. "See how warm and tired you are!"

"I do not mind," she said.

"Still, she is quite heavy," he replied. "As I turned and saw you," he continued, "with the baby's arms clasped around your neck, I was reminded of my first meeting with you. Do you remember?"

"Distinctly," she replied. And had Ralph looked down into that sweet, blushing face, he could not have failed to read her secret. But he did not. Just ahead stood Dora, and unconsciously he hurried his footsteps; but a slight

flash of self-reproach went through his mind, as
he realized how his love had made him forgetful
of Jean's sweet friendship, which he had at one
time so appreciated, and for which he had been
so thankful in his earlier days of loneliness and
depression.

"I, for one, shall never forget it," he continued after a pause, a pause not noted by Jean
in her intense enjoyment of the moment.   The
pleasure of his coming forward to help her had
set her quiet little heart to beating wildly, so that
she could hardly speak, and this short pause
gave her time to recover a little of her self-control.

"I think you are my 'mascot' and have brought
me luck, and if all goes as well as I wish," he
added, "I shall have cause to thank you all my
life, for through you has come the greatest joy of
my life."

They had now overtaken the others, and Jean
could not reply, even had she been able to do so.

Dora gave one quick, searching look into
Jean's face, and felt that something wonderful
had taken place, for it was indeed "a face illumined"—illumined with a great and holy
love.   As Dora looked, a fierce, keen pang shot
through her heart.   What could Ralph have been
saying to cause that sweet, gentle face she had so
lovingly held between her hands and called
"placid" to become almost beautiful from the
love-light in the eyes, the bright flush on the
usually pale face, and the new expression on the
sweet mouth?   Why should she care? she told

herself, as she turned quickly and walked on ahead. Again she thought of the look upon Ralph's face, and she remembered that, before entering the room, he had held a few moments' conversation in a low tone with Jean in the hall. Could it be possible that he loved Jean, and that it was the love for Jean she had seen in his face as he came toward her? Then for the first time she realized that she had always given him the preference in her heart, at least, and she understood now what had caused her emotion as he had held her hands and looked into her face the night before.

"She should never betray herself again," she resolved, and she determined to use every means in her power to prove to Ralph that she did not love him.

Acting upon this, she became gayer than ever, and seemed like a bright butterfly as she fluttered along, now looking into the old open fireplace in the old kitchen, now running her fingers lightly over the old harpsichord in the parlor; rushing from room to room, in apparent delight, never giving Ralph a moment to linger by her side; in fact leaving him alone with Jean at every opportunity.

Once she evaded them all entirely, and finding herself alone, she sank down in a chair in the room in which Washington had breathed his last, and there, in the shelter of that old armchair which had no doubt held many another sorrowing

heart, she wrestled with the good and bad promptings of her heart.

Why should she yield him up so tamely? she
told herself; for in spite of what she believed to
be the truth, something seemed to whisper that
she might yet win him if she chose. Now that
she realized that she loved him, and although she
had avoided him for the last two hours, she had
cast many a glance toward him, and never had he
seemed so tall and handsome, so attractive in his
youthful, manly beauty, as now that she feared
he was indifferent toward her—and yet she could
not quite believe that the latter was true.

When she at first sank into that old armchair
she felt very wretched and unhappy; but as she
listened to the soft music of hope which told her
she might yet win his love, and recalled many
words and glances in the past few weeks which
gave the lie to her doubts, the smiles returned to
her face, and turning her head toward the window, she looked out upon the lovely view beyond,
but saw it not, saw only life as she would like it
to be, in a sweet dream of the future. She had
been in a state of excitement ever since the early
morning. She was tired physically and men-
tally, and in a few minutes was fast asleep.

She was not allowed to remain alone very
long, for she was soon awakened by Jean calling
her from the garden, they having just seen her
asleep by the window. As she looked out and
saw Jean's smiling face she realized that, although she might have a doubt as to whom Ralph

really loved, she had none as to Jean's state of mind, and all the tenderness she had felt that morning toward her friend seemed to pass away, and in its place a cold, hard feeling took possession of her, which lasted through many days, and which built up a barrier that nearly wrecked her life.

When she joined the others, they laughed at her thus falling asleep, but she complained of not feeling well; and as they were all somewhat exhausted, the change in her face and spirits passed unnoticed by all except Ralph, and he feared it was of Delacy she was thinking, as she sat so quiet all the way home, looking out over the water with a cold, disconsolate look. The soft, lovely mouth, so easily curved into smiles, was shut tightly and drawn a little at the corners. The lids fell heavily over the bright, sparkling eyes, with a look that pained him as he noticed their hard, cold glitter. She had always appeared to him as the embodiment of light and sunshine, and he felt for the first time that she might be hard and cruel. But he was too much in love to allow this more than a passing thought. He felt that something had made her unhappy and this drew from him all the tenderness of love's wish to console her, or share her sorrow. All else was quickly forgotten.

To Jean the day had been perfect, not a cloud had dimmed its brightness, and she felt that God had numbered her among the blessed.

Over and over she said to herself, "Through

you has come the greatest joy of my life." How
natural that she should put her own construction
upon this! How was she to know that, because
of her kindness to Dora, and thus bringing her
into his life, he should feel his greatest gratitude toward her?

With all his love for Dora, he was well aware
that, simply meeting her unknown at Mrs. Graham's, things would have been different.

He had become interested in her through Jean,
even before he met her, and through the knowledge thus obtained he was able to believe in her
from the first.

Jean could not forget the tenderness in his
voice. She felt she could not be wrong in putting the interpretation she wished upon his
words.

Deep would have been Ralph's sorrow had he
known how his words appeared to her, and what
false hopes they built in her loving heart.

CHAPTER XIX

RALPH felt that it was for the best that he had
not been left alone with Dora during the whole
day, for he knew it would have been very hard
for him not to tell her of his love, and so when
reporting for work he was rather glad when told
that his duties would take him away from the city
at once.

As "Special Agent" he was sent to certain
land offices in the West on business for the Department. His route lay through the city which
was Delacy's home, and this added to his satis-
faction at leaving Washington at this time, as he
would thus be able to see and have an understanding with Delacy.

When he called at Jim's to bid them all good-
bye, he found them all sitting out in the little
front yard which had so lately been added to the
house, by the Board of Public Works, in their
new plans for beautifying the city, and which
made such a delightfully cool spot in which to
linger on this warm evening.

All were sorry that Ralph was to leave them
so suddenly. While Jim and Marie did most of
the talking during his call, Ralph had much to
say as to his plans for the future. He told Jim
that his first talk after his arrival at Washington

had not been forgotten, and that he had thought seriously upon what he had said about studying law, and making his appointment here only a stepping-stone to something higher in life. He regretted that the position to which he had been appointed prevented his immediately entering the law school here, but it was beneficial, inasmuch as it would give him some idea of the West and the best place in which to locate when he was ready to resign, after having become a full-fledged lawyer.

He talked to Jim, but his words were meant for other ears. He talked as he had never talked before of his hopes, his plans, his ambitions; all but his love was laid before them in hopes that the right one might know and understand him better, and many times he told them that until he returned to them he would be discontented and unhappy, for so dear had they all become that he would be homesick for them until he was with them once again; and so he took his leave, telling both girls that he would be braver and better if they would write to him. This they both consented to do.

After having shaken hands with all, he turned again to Dora, and, taking her hand, he held it for a few minutes tightly in his own, and whispered softly, "God bless you!" and unable to say another word, hurried out through the little gate.

Dora and Jean had little to say to each other that night during their undressing, and each in her own heart was glad that the other was silent.

Jean was very unhappy at this sudden departure of one who had grown so dear to her, and Dora because of the uncertain emotions this last pressure of the hands, and softly whispered words, had awakened in her.

Ever since her trip down the river she had been in a terribly restless, uncertain state of mind. She had received the letter from Delacy, and as he had all but told of his love, she had tried to find consolation in the thought that some one loved her at least, if Ralph did not. She might be able to do so, she thought, could she only convince herself that Ralph really was in love with Jean. She endeavored to draw a confession from Jean that might satisfy her on this point, but as Jean had nothing to tell, she was as much in the dark as ever.

This uncertainty made her nervous and restless, and her pride and anger at giving her love unasked made her harder to get along with than ever. She began to feel a recklessness of conduct and of consequences that boded no good to herself or others. She had not entirely overcome her recent hard feelings toward Jean, who could not account for this coldness, and tried her best to overcome it in her sweet, gentle way, but this very gentleness and peace seemed only to provoke Dora to greater unkindness.

Jean would not be so calm and gentle, she thought, if she were not happy, and sure of Ralph's love, and this suspicion prevented Jean's advances from restoring their late friendship.

She missed the attention of the young men and the many gay times they had all enjoyed together. Always fond of life and pleasure, her evenings seemed more than dull; they now appeared unbearable. In her discontent she made Jean unhappy (who began to feel almost sorry that she roomed so near), as all her quiet evenings were thus spoiled by Dora's restlessness. Her work each day seemed more objectionable, and all the dislike for such a life returned stronger than ever, and she felt that she would welcome any change that would deliver her from it. Her work was light, and she did less of it than ever, spending most of her time standing by the open window, looking out upon the fountain and the White House, and envying those who were free to walk about in that fair park.

The Prominent Official had not ceased his attentions to her. He had come nearly every day to her desk, and finding her often by the open window, he would linger and cultivate her discontent.

She laughed when Jean warned her about this and against him. He was old enough to be her father, she said, although this was not true. He was just in the prime of life, fairly good-looking, tall and slender as a young man, with reddish mustache, and the only thing that Dora had to found such an assertion upon was his bald forehead. But this does not always come from age. He was very kind to her and had completely won her confidence and trust. He helped to make

her days pass quickly, and she realized that
through his influence she was allowed to do pretty
much as she pleased, and for this she felt grateful. She was not thoughtful enough to see that
he pampered all her faults and appealed only to
her baser emotions. She only felt that he always
agreed with her mood and made her feel herself
right when conscience would have perhaps told
her the truth.

In her present mood, she turned toward him
more than ever. He was the only congenial spirit,
she felt, left her. But for him she would have
been more miserable, she thought, though but for
him she would have been soothed by Jean's gentle influence in a little while, but every day she
carried home in her heart some little seed of discontent which he had planted.

That her intimacy with him might cause talk,
she cared but little. She had been raised on the
borderland of Bohemia, where an innocent girl
gains a certain amount of knowledge of the evils
of the world, without fully comprehending them;
therefore she was indifferent as to what people
might say, and that such talk could ever perma-
nently harm her never entered her head.

Both Mrs. Graham and the Prominent Official
were not slow to notice the change in Dora, and
as Dora's friendship for Jean was now tinged
with doubt and half envy or jealousy, she of her
own accord sought Mrs. Graham in preference
to Jean on her walks from the office. Thus she
opened the door to the demon, "Don't care," who,

when he has once put his foot over the threshold, soon owns the whole edifice, and with "What's the difference?" ruins all within.

Why should she not have all the enjoyment out of her dull life she could get? It was hard enough to work at all, day after day, in a close room, and then never having any fun or pleasure of an evening was more than she was willing to endure.

It was tiresome home alone with Jean evening after evening. She was very sweet and nice, but terribly dull. Mrs. Graham was much more fun, and the Prominent Official better than no one to flirt with, and why should she care if a lot of dull, stupid people shook their heads at them? She had never seen or heard them do anything wrong. If Delacy and Ralph were not on hand to amuse her, why should she not get all the amusement she could from those who were anxious to please her?

She became tired of being quiet, and truly of her it might be said: "Quiet to quick bosoms is a hell, and there has been thy bane." So when Mrs. Graham asked her to join a party to go over to Baltimore she was delighted.

Jean was not so taken up with her own thoughts but that she was conscious of a change in Dora, and worried over it a good deal. All the interest she had ever felt was intensified since she had become an inmate in the same house, and she had grown to love her very dearly.

She had received long, interesting descriptive

letters from Ralph, and in each one he had asked
her not to lose interest in her dear friend Dora,
but to shield her with all her power from harm—
or some such words, that always left her more anxious than ever to watch over and shield her friend
from those whose acquaintance she felt would
only lead Dora in harm's way.

When Dora told her of the trip to Baltimore,
how they were going over after office hours, and,
after a drive in the park, to take dinner at the
hotel, returning on the last train, Jean felt that
in such company there was danger for Dora and
said all she could to persuade her to give it up;
but Dora was obstinate, and nothing she could
say would turn her.

"What harm can there be in my going with
Mrs. Graham and her friends ?" she asked.

"There would not be any harm if it was not
with Mrs. Graham and her friends," replied
Jean.

"You are always talking about Mrs. Graham.
What do you really know against her ?"

"That is hard to answer. Of my personal
knowledge I know nothing, and still——"

"There, that is just it," interrupted Dora.
"You know nothing except the gossip of the
office. It does not seem like you, Jean, to found
your opinion of a person on what other people
say. Of course, they are all jealous of her at the
office. She is handsome and stylish, and has
strong influence enough to allow her to act with
perfect independence."

"That is not entirely true, Dora. I have been longer in the same room with her than you, and I have formed my own estimation of her character, and I certainly do not think her a safe friend for you."

"I am afraid you are narrow, Jean. Why, I do not believe you have ever exchanged half a dozen words with her, while I have. She is a very attractive woman, and I see no harm in her friendship, but much to be gained by it. She is acquainted with some of the most prominent people here."

"Of the male sex, perhaps."

"Well, no doubt they find her, as I do, very attractive, and I say again, I see no harm in going over to Baltimore with her. Can you really tell me a good reason why I should not go?"

"I must confess, Dora, that I am guided simply by my feelings in the matter. I may be prejudiced against her; still, where there is a doubt upon such a subject, it is best to be on the safe side. It is nearly always the first step that counts; it is always harder to turn back. You might take this trip and nothing harmful come of it, and then it might ruin your whole life. The barriers that arise in our way often seem like garlands of finest flowers, which would only be a pleasure to sever; but if we break through them they often leave a poisonous stain that years will never wash clean. I am no older than you, Dora, but I have had two years' experience in

office work, and I have had an aunt who left her
experience to me as her only wealth."

"I must have my own experience in life; I
cannot take that of others. You have your inner
promptings, I have mine, and mine tell me I am
tired of working all day, and nothing to do of an
evening. I cannot be like you, contented with a
book for an evening's excitement. I am not as
weak as you think. I, too, have a certain knowledge of life, although different from yours, and I
think I am able to take care of myself."

The very knowledge that she ought not to go
made her more determined to do so, and added
spice to the already exciting anticipation of a
change from the quiet life she had been having
since the young men left the city.

The plans were made, the day set, and although Jean talked and coaxed and pleaded, she
only laughed and called her a little goose, just as
though she could not take care of herself, she always added.

Jean left her that morning at the iron gate
with a heavy heart, though just why she could
not tell. She felt that Dora needed a change
and constant excitement to make her happy, and
the trip in itself might do her good, but she had
no confidence in Mrs. Graham, and the reputation
of the Prominent Official was too well known to
have a doubt about. To add to her fear, she received a long letter from Ralph in which he again
spoke of Dora, of her great beauty and the temptation it exposed her to, of the influence for good

he believed Jean to have over her, and beseeching Jean not to relax in her efforts to shield her from harm with all the means in her power.

She took her seat before the stack of mutilated sheets, opened her package of perfect ones to exchange for the torn or soiled ones the counters would bring her, but her mind was disturbed and her heart full of prayers for Dora.

Over and over she repeated those words of Ralph's, "Leave no stone unturned to keep her from harm, for my sake."

Here was Dora in danger, she felt sure, and she powerless to help her, while Ralph had confidence in her ability to do so, and would perhaps blame her if any injury to Dora should result from this little frolic.

"For his sake," he had said. Of course, he meant that should she fail to do so he would be disappointed in her. She could not bear the thought of this, so she again determined that she must save her at all cost. Then she took herself to task. Perhaps she had not done all in her power. Was there not something still that she might say or do to persuade her not to go? She would see her at twelve o'clock and try once more.

The morning dragged terribly, and her head began to ache until she could hardly see what she was doing.

So when the bell rang for noon, she hurried into Dora's room and found her talking with Mrs. Graham.

"You will surely be at the depot in time,"

Jean heard Mrs. Graham say, as she walked up to Dora's desk.

"Yes, I will come just as soon as I can get out," replied Dora. Her face was flushed, but as she saw Jean a look of determination came over it. She began to fret against Jean's interference.

Once again Mrs. Graham gave Jean a triumphant look, and Jean felt her helplessness more than ever, but that look also stirred in Jean a heroic determination to prevent Dora's going at all hazards.

Mrs. Graham had on her bonnet, and again charging Dora not to miss the train, left for home, as she told Dora that she would need the afternoon to rest for their evening's frolic. As she left Dora's desk Jean again began her pleading, but in vain. Dora said she had promised to meet Mrs. Graham at the depot at five o'clock, and she would do so.

Again Jean resumed her work; this time her eyes were blinded with tears, and her hand trembled, and before she knew it she had passed two sheets for one, and so grieving and worrying, she counted and exchanged sheets.

In a little while, when she came to balance up her mutilated sheets, she found she was one sheet short of a hundred. She had time to rectify it and was about to do so, and arose to have her last package of work brought back, but as she did so it flashed across her mind that here was a chance of saving Dora.

It was an ironclad rule in those days that when any work was found wrong at the end of the afternoon in any division, no one could leave the Bureau until the mistake was rectified.

Mrs. Graham had left the office at twelve, and Dora was to meet her and the rest of the party at the depot. Could she be detained if only for an hour, she would miss the train, and they would go without her.

All this flashed through Jean's mind as she arose to rectify her mistake, which she could easily do, as her work was all on the table beside her, not having been sent from the room to the vault, as it would be in a short time.

Should she do it? She grasped the edge of the table for support, she felt so very faint.

She sat down for an instant to think. Should she let her work be put away with the rest of the work of that division, which the messengers were already beginning to put once more in those long trunk-like boxes, and carrying out of the room to be put in the vault, to be carried the next morning to another division, where it would be stamped or sealed, or numbered, as the case might be, on its journey to completion? Should she let hers go, at the end of the evening her work would come out incorrect, her number of mutilated and number of perfect sheets not making an even thousand, as they should do. They would not know where the mistake was. All the work would have to be counted until it was found.

As she carried on the interchange of good

sheets for bad, with others, it was liable to happen in several ways. She might have given three for two and they not have noticed the difference, or some of the packages might have been wrong when given to her.

She was one of the most skilful and careful counters in the whole Bureau. They would naturally look for it first among the work of others. Of course it would be found. But it was her duty to report the mistake as soon as she discovered one had been made. She blushed to think of the shame she should feel when the error was discovered, but they would never know that she let it pass when she could have rectified it.

The messenger came to the table to take her work. Should she let it go? Mrs. Graham's triumphant smile arose before her eyes. Ralph's faith that she would save Dora if she could, rushed through her mind.

In trembling tones she told him it might all be put away. She watched it put in the box with other packages piled upon it; she saw them carry it out of the room and as though they were carrying out a corpse—her dead reputation. She arose as though to call them back, and fell to the floor in a dead faint.

"Alas! how often does goodness wound itself,
    And sweet affection prove the spring of woe!"

It was not an unusual thing for those hard-

worked women in those illy ventilated rooms to
faint at their work, and Jean was soon on the
lounge in the dressing-room, receiving the tender
nursing of several willing hands, and after resting a little while she insisted upon resuming her
work. At a quarter of four she walked up to the
Superintendent's desk, as well as her trembling
limbs would carry her, and in faltering tones
and with a sad, pale face told her that her work
was one sheet short.

Such an announcement at so late an hour always caused a certain commotion. Many had
already finished their work. Some had their
wraps on, ready to leave at the ringing of the
gong at the iron gate which told that all was over
for the day. Others were washing their sponges,
so that in the morning they would need only a
mere wetting to start work; others who were
more careless left them full of the green stains
which the fingers had transferred from the fresh
green ink on the back of the notes to the wet
sponges as they moistened the tips of the fingers
to turn the edge of the sheets.

As the day's work had all been finished, and
the messengers were carrying it out to the vault
where all work had to be stored for the night,
each Superintendent signing the work of her
division as correct, or if, as it now happened, a
mistake was found, then all the day's work in
that division had to be recounted until the error
was discovered.

Miss Temple gave the order for the work to be

brought back. All resumed their seats to begin
counting. How their fingers flew over the quickly
turned sheets! Each counter took a package, and
as they were not to look for torn, soiled or mis-
printed ones, they were able to make very quick
time over their count. It was almost as much as
the messengers could do to tie and untie the packages so as to keep them supplied with work. All
was hurry. All wanted to get home. All were
more or less afraid that the mistake would be
found in their work, and Jean felt all this as she
sat with her bowed head and guilty heart, so full
of grief that to save one wilful girl she was keeping hundreds from going home.

Miss Temple, seeing how pale she was, and
how ill she had been during the afternoon, would
not let her help to find the mistake, but told her
to rest. This she was only too glad to do, so she
rested her arms on the table before her and buried
her face therein.

Outside the room, in all the other divisions
they were sitting around waiting, men and
women, for until the key of each division was in
the place and the vault closed and locked, no one
could leave.

Would it be in vain? Jean kept saying to herself. Would they find it in time for Dora to
catch the train after all? How mortified she
would be when her name was passed from one to
another as having made a mistake in her work,
and her reputation as a skilled worker ruined!
What was to keep her in her position now? She

had no influence and never had any. She had obtained the place made vacant by the death of her aunt through the kindness of the Chief of the Bureau. There were rumors of a big discharge to take place soon. As she would be proven a careless worker, what was to retain her, should the Chief no longer see fit to do so? Never did she forget in all her life that hour of bitter suffering. Again did her slight strength fail her and she became unconscious, but as she rested upon the table no one noticed her.

At last she was aroused by the gentle touch of Miss Temple's hand, and she knew it had been found.

"Did you find it?" she asked in a whisper, her voice was so weak.

"Yes, and it was in your work; but do not feel badly about it, dear. You have been ill all day, and I should have made you go home instead of letting you try to work."

At her kind words Jean sought a woman's refuge in tears, and when she had recovered sufficiently to go home, she found that she and Miss Temple were about the last to leave the office. She did not know whether she had been successful in saving Dora or not. Miss Temple, seeing how weak and unnerved she was, went all the way home with her, and Marie soon had her cuddled into bed, upon hearing how sick she had been all day.

CHAPTER XX

When Dora found they were to be delayed in getting out she regretted she had not left earlier in the afternoon. The Prominent Official had not been at the office all day, or she would have gotten him to obtain a pass from the chief, and they could have left together. The clerks alone were sometimes allowed this privilege, but it required a certain amount of red tape even for these favorites of fortune to accomplish it. So Dora had to make the best of it, and sat waiting with the rest, with all the limited amount of patience she could summon to her control.

Never did an evening's pleasure seem so desirable as this, which she feared, owing to this delay, would now become an impossibility. She ran each of the delightful details over in her mind. An hour's ride in the cars, a carriage to meet them at the depot, and then an hour's drive in the beautiful Druid Hill Park on this lovely evening. An hour for dinner, with everything in season that was good to eat; then, best of all, an evening of opera. Summer opera, it is true, but no less delightful to Dora in anticipation. Then a hurry to take the midnight train. Such a rush of events as she loved. If on her very first

164

day Dora felt she was in prison, how must it have been with her now? She was sure that no convict condemned for a long term of years could feel worse than she did. How she longed for freedom of action and independence to do as she pleased! She had a strong desire to take up the long ruler on her desk and beat her way out past the jailer at the strong iron gates.

Instead, she was obliged to sit silently in her chair and wait until the gong sounded, which it did at half-past five.

There was just one chance left. As she had failed to meet them at the five o'clock train, Mrs. Graham might not have gone, as she had said she would not go without her. If she had returned to her hotel, they might still be in time to take a later train. They would miss their drive, and perhaps hurry dinner, but they would be in time for the theatre. After all, the latter was the great attraction to Dora. As the hotel was near the Treasury, Dora reached it in a few minutes. She did not wait to send up her card, but ran quickly up to her room. Tapping on the door, she was bidden to enter.

She had been in hopes of finding her; but she did not expect to see her in negligée costume, reclining upon a lounge, book in hand, and a stout negress at the head of the couch, fanning and drying her luxurious tresses, while beside her stood all the necessary articles for a shampoo.

It was very evident that she had not just returned, for her long, thick hair was nearly dry.

She jumped up in surprise when she saw Dora.
"Did he not meet you ?" she exclaimed.

"I have met no one," said Dora. "We were
detained at the office until just now."

"Then you did not go to the depot ?"

"No; I came here first to see if you had returned; but I see you did not go at all."

They were still standing—Dora, tall, erect,
with the proud, haughty head, and the imperious
manner of a young princess; Mrs. Graham, as
tall, but her fine figure was more round, fuller
and lacked the slender grace of youth. All around
her swept her magnificent hair, nearly reaching
to the floor in a mass of fragrant electrified waves
from its recent bath and brushing. Behind her
stood the negress with a towel over her arm, and
a large palm-leaf fan in her hand.

Dora looked at Mrs. Graham with a surprised,
searching glance, but Mrs. Graham did not return the look—the long, fringed lashes were
drooped over the cold gray eyes, and her mobile
mouth assumed a sad expression.

"I had a terrible headache come on me this
afternoon, and found I would not be able to go.
As the rest were to meet you at the depot, and
take care of you, I thought I would not be missed.
I felt so badly I sent for Nancy here to see if
she could not cure this terrible headache, but she
has hardly been successful," and she put her fine
white hand up to her temples as though in great
pain. "Nancy, you may wait in the other room,"
she turned and said to the waiting maid.

"I am sorry for your headache," said Dora; "pray, lie down again; I fear I have disturbed you. Of course I would not have gone without you, as all are strangers except 'Our Mutual Friend," for thus Mrs. Graham always spoke of the Prominent Official to Dora.

"I am sorry to have spoiled your pleasure, and he will be more so. He is very fond of you, Dora, and has set his heart upon a whole evening with you. I fear he will scold me terribly. You had better remain here; for if he finds we do not come, he will probably come here to find out the reason. Then I will find my poor head worse from the scolding I shall get for having made a mess of his well-laid plans for a delightful evening."

"You forget that I was prevented from going by a mistake at the office. You have only to tell him that. But he has no doubt gone over with the others."

"He would not go without you, Dora; of that I am certain. You, and you alone, are the attraction to him. Come, take off your things. He will come here, I am sure, and we will try to forget our disappointment of an evening in Baltimore."

"And your headache?" asked Dora.

"Oh, Nancy will have cured it by that time," she said, with some confusion.

Mrs. Graham half lifted those white eyelids, and, looking through her long lashes, watched Dora while she hesitated, for a few minutes, unobserved. Seeing no signs of her yielding, she continued in her soft, low tones:

"Is it so much to ask, that you hesitate? One evening to give to me and the friend who has done so much for you, and is so willing to do more? I should not like to think you ungrateful." And Mrs. Graham turned away from Dora and seated herself in one of the big armchairs with which the room was bountifully supplied.

"Oh, Mrs. Graham," said Dora, and, kneeling by her side, she threw her arms around her, "do not say that; have I not shown my friendship for you in spite of everything?"

"Everything, I suppose, means the 'little dragon'," referring to Jean. "I am well aware she leaves no stone unturned to break our friendship. But it is not to me alone, Dora, that you owe gratitude, and in persuading you to remain it is not simply for my own pleasure, but for one who has been patient in waiting for some acknowledgment of all he has done for you."

Dora did not see where she was wanting in this quality; in fact, it was not numbered among her many failings. She was more inclined to go to the other extreme. She therefore felt a little hurt that it should be attributed to her.

"I assure you I am grateful, and I try each day to show my appreciation of both your kindness and his. What other acknowledgment can he want of me, and in what have I failed to show it?"

Mrs. Graham answered only the last of this remark.

"I do not say you *have failed* at all; only, as you hesitated to remain and spend the evening with us, I said I should 'hate to think you ungrateful.' Have you forgotten our first pleasant evening here together ?"

This was an unfortunate reference, for Dora, having no valid reason, was about to remain.

After all, Jean's long talks and good counsels had not been in vain. As Mrs. Graham referred to that first evening in her room, it all came back to her vividly, not in the light in which it had at first appeared, but as Jean had taught her to consider it. Involuntarily, her eyes wandered to the corner where she and Ralph had passed their first evening together, and over her rushed the full force of the love she felt for him.

Somehow, she felt no inclination to spend the evening so near that sacred spot. She also had received a letter from Ralph that day, and hope was now uppermost. "Please do not think me rude or ungrateful, but I feel I cannot remain this evening. The excitement of waiting to get out of the office has given me a headache. I feel disappointed, cross, and in no mood to give either of you a happy evening. You do not know me," she continued quickly, seeing Mrs. Graham about to speak. "I am like the little girl—'when I am good, I am very, very good; when I am bad, I am horrid.' Let me come some other evening, when I am in a merry mood, and then I will show my gratitude; but as I feel now, I should only disappoint you both."

Mrs. Graham, thinking perhaps this would be best, and feeling no real interest in it, satisfied that she had done what she could for the Prominent Official, let her go; and Dora, hardly knowing why she had been obstinate, hurried towards home, the interview with Mrs. Graham having lasted about half an hour.

She was walking quickly up Fourteenth street, when she was surprised by seeing the Prominent Official jump from a car and hasten towards her just as she was about to enter Franklin Square.

"How fortunate!" he said. "A few minutes later and I should have missed you. Why did you not keep your appointment?"

"We were kept at the office, through some mistake," she answered.

"Why did I not think of that," he said, "and have you excused early? Well, as I have found you, all may yet be right, after all. When you did not come I was in despair. Mrs. Graham and the others left; but I remained behind to bring you over in a later train."

"Mrs. Graham!" exclaimed Dora. They were walking now side by side and were nearing the fountain in the center.

"Yes," he replied; "she said you must not think hard of her going without you, because she feared, as you had not come, that you had changed your mind and were not going, so she concluded to go on with the others. But I knew better; I felt sure you would come, but when you did not I determined to go for you, even up to the 'dragon's' den, to coax you to go with me in a later train. I was just on my way to your house when I saw you from the car."

"Mrs. Graham has gone to Baltimore, you say?" said Dora, and unconsciously she stopped still by the edge of the fountain.

"Of course; I put her on the five o'clock train myself. You will come with me, will you not? We will miss our drive, but we can get part of the dinner, and hear the opera, and if we hurry we will have time to catch the next train. Do not refuse me this, Dora," and he laid his hand lightly on her arm.

He had talked quickly; he thought by her manner that she was offended by Mrs. Graham going without her. As he stood there, looking into her beautiful face, all the passion with which her beauty had inspired him, and which he had controlled for so long, filled him with the determination to risk all in his effort to win her. He must get her to go to Baltimore; once there he had laid his plans so well that the rest would be easy. He was therefore much surprised when she said with suppressed passion:

"I have just left Mrs. Graham!"

"The devil!" he exclaimed.

"He is here beside me, I think."

It was nearly dark, and but few people were passing through the park. As Dora made the last remark she turned and walked quickly from him.

With a few strides he was again by her side. He grasped her hand and stopped her.

"Do not go from me yet, Dora, I beg of you. Listen to me for a few moments, I implore you. I will tell you all, and then you can judge me. Why hide it from you longer?—I love you. I worship you. Ever since I first looked upon your face I have been bewitched by your beauty and longed to clasp you in my arms."

Dora tried to get her hand away, but he held her tight.

"How dare you, sir," she cried, "when I trusted you, and looked upon you as a benefactor —nay, a friend? You, a man with a wife, to speak to me of love!"

"The Courts of Love decided in the Middle Ages that being married did not prevent one from falling in love with some one else. I have never troubled you with my domestic affairs, or you would have known that there is no love in our household. And all that my heart has had for many a day has been yours. I have a wife, it is true, but she is such only in name. Our paths have been separate ones for many years. And it needs only a few words to sever the tie forever. You have come into my life like a ray of sunshine on a cloudy day. To-night I had planned to tell you all, but not in this abrupt way, which, I know, has startled you. Do not think I wished to insult you by offering you this love until I am free to do so. All I wished was that you might know it; that in your inmost thought some sweet tenderness might be given with your friendship for me. Man was made for love, and seek it he must at home or abroad, and as I am not at present in a position to seek your love I simply desired to tell you of mine, that you might look upon me as something more than a friend to you. Knowing this, will you not forgive me for lying to you just now, for planning to get you all to myself this evening that I might tell you of my hopes and plans for the future ?"

He tried to draw her nearer that he might put his arm around her waist, but Dora drew away with such a haughty look that he feared to spoil the good impression he hoped he was making, although he longed with beating pulse to clasp her in his arms.

"Then Mrs. Graham never intended going ?" she asked.

He thought it best to tell her the whole truth now.

"No; I was to meet you at the train and tell you that she was on board with the rest, and you and I were to enter the car; and as they would not be there, I was to go and see where they had moved to, and when I returned to you the train would be moving, and I was to tell you that while waiting for you the first section of the train, in which they happened to be seated, had gone on ahead."

"And when we got to Baltimore ?"

Her calmness threw him off his guard. Certainly Dora was no timid doe, and the knowledge of life as she had thus far learned it helped her at last to read this man aright.

"We would have carried out our programme just as we planned it, only you and I would have enjoyed it alone together. Come, it is not too late. Show me that you are still my friend by going with me."

Dora raised her small, white hand and slapped him squarely in the mouth.

"You scoundrel!" she exclaimed, and ran swiftly from him out into the street.

He saw it would attract too much attention to follow her, so, swearing heartily at his ill luck, he retraced his steps to vent his rage upon Mrs. Graham. He put his hand to his mouth.

"The delicious little devil!" he said, and smiled. Had a man given the blow nought but rage and revenge would have filled his mind; but this very of Dora only drew him nearer to her, and changed his anger to the enjoyment of her spunk and temper. He never enjoyed an easy conquest.

Dora ran quickly along until within a few squares of her home, when, making sure that he was not near, she walked slowly to recover her breath and some composure of manner.

On entering the house she found the doctor had been sent for by Jim, for Jean, who had become delirious with fever, so her excited appearance was, therefore, overlooked, for which she was thankful.

She begged to be allowed to sit up with Jean all night, and Marie at last consented to yield her place to her.

As she sat there alone with Jean, and heard her rave of "lost sheets" and repeat over and over again, "It was to save Dora"—"It was for Ralph's sake," she realized what she had done.

She had time to think of many things, and most of all from what Jean had saved her—a lost reputation, at least.

With face hidden in the bed-clothes, she shed many bitter tears as she realized how wilful and careless she had been. Never again, she determined, would she set up her own wishes before all else.

She was filled with many emotions—gratitude to Jean; anger at the conduct of the Prominent Official, who had gained her friendship through his kindness and whom she had considered a sort of protector; while towards Mrs. Graham, who had taken such an active part in the trap set for her, and whom she had fancied in her impulsive way, she felt great indignation and anger, mingled with a disappointment and sorrow from which it would be hard to recover. Such a shock to a young, trusting heart is not soon forgotten, although with Dora's impulsive temperament it was more than liable to occur again. Yet at first it might make her a little more careful in selecting her friends and mistrustful of those whom she met.

But for the first time she felt her weakness in

this direction, and realized that she needed a stronger will than her own to control her.

She was heartily ashamed of the way she had felt and acted towards Jean since the day at Mount Vernon, and was anxious to show the gratitude she felt for what she had done, and determined to avail herself of the first opportunity to offer her sacrifice upon the altar of friendship.

Jean alone was worthy of Ralph, and she would tear her love for him from her heart and make not the slightest effort to win him for herself.

Jean was better the next day, but Dora remained at home to nurse her, and was as gentle and tender as Jean herself could have been.

That afternoon, while sitting beside the bed, Jean asked, with a flushed face and nervous manner, "Did you go?"

"No," replied Dora; "I missed the train, and, Jean, dear, I am so glad"; and she put her head down beside Jean's on the pillow, in order to hide her face, as she did not think it best to tell all to Jean in her weakened state.

"I am so glad, dear," said Jean, and a peaceful, happy look stole over her face, and she was soon in a sweet sleep.

Dora remained home with Jean for the rest of the week, but neither referred to the subject again for many days.

CHAPTER XXI

WHEN Dora returned to the office, after nursing Jean for nearly a week, she was met at the iron gate by the Prominent Official, who seemed to be waiting there for her. She looked him full in the face, but, much to the surprise of those standing near, passed on with neither a bow nor a smile. He flushed a little, turned quickly and went up the steps leading to the floor above.

Dora walked to her desk with a little feeling of triumph mingled with her anger toward him. She was glad the others had seen her cut him, little thinking that it could only add gossip to those who had watched her intimacy with him. The look of vexation she saw upon his face satisfied her that she had annoyed him. She was not at her desk very long before she received the following note from him:

"Day after day have I watched for your return, that I might see upon your face some sign of forgiveness. Could you know how worried and grieved I have been for fear you were ill, I am sure your kind heart would grant me what I ask—forgiveness—even if you can no longer call me friend. The sorrow I feel at having lost this place in your affection is greater than all the sorrows of my life, which have been many. Let me come and hear you say that you forgive me, and I will patiently wait until I can redeem myself in your estimation. I promise not to annoy you or intrude myself upon you, if you will but grant me this request."

"I can neither forgive nor forget," was Dora's reply.

For several days Dora heard nothing more from him; although each morning he stood near the gate and saw her enter, she passed him without a glance, with a proud head upheld, which seemed to give her a dignity and self-possession beyond her years. She was annoyed that he should so persist in thus intruding himself upon her. Mrs. Graham she had not seen. She wrote her a note telling her she knew the part she had taken, and how pained she had been to find out that she had been such a false friend to her, and that their acquaintance must never be renewed. Mrs. Graham cared little about this, as she had entered into the whole thing to please the Prominent Official, and was rather glad than otherwise that it had turned out as it did, through no fault of hers, but the blunders of others. She had her own plans and schemes in life, in which Dora formed no part, and she felt that Dora was too beautiful to keep near her if she wished them to succeed.

Thus things went on for about a week, when a new turn was given by Dora finding upon her desk one morning the following note:

"I have watched each day for a sign of relenting on your face, and have come to the conclusion that you mean what you say. I am sorry you force me to extreme measures. You seem to forget that those who elevate can also reduce. I have also found out who made the mistake which prevented your leaving the office at four. You have no doubt heard of the big discharge which takes place in a few days. Perhaps what you will not do for me you will for the sake of your friend. Remember, all I ask is that you forgive me. I leave on my vacation in a few days, but will not go without the one word from you."

All Dora's indignation and anger awoke afresh at the reading of this letter. For herself, Dora had no fear, and the loss of her position would have been looked upon as a relief, but she knew well what such a discharge would be to Jean.

Jean had sacrificed herself to save her, and surely she ought to be willing to do what she could to turn away his wrath from her; therefore she answered and said:

"I will try to forgive."

And he wrote back and said:

"If you try you will succeed, and it will not be my fault if you do not forget. Let me come and say 'good-bye,' and then you will not be troubled with me for weeks to come."

Not waiting for a reply, he was soon by her desk. His manner was well assumed to throw her off her guard; his words few and such as the whole world might hear. She felt as he left her

that she had taught him a lesson that he would
not forget, and as they did not meet again for
some time, her anger towards him had time to
cool.

Thus Dora opened the door to future trouble.
The summer exodus, which was more general in
those days than it is now, had begun, and every
one able to do so left the city. All the clerks have
a month's leave with pay. They are also allowed
thirty days' sick leave during the year. If they
can save these by fair means or foul, they often
add them to their vacation time, and if they can
afford it, as such as Mrs. Graham felt they could,
they took a month without pay added to that,
thus getting three months' leave, losing only one
month's salary.

Dora, who since her promotion to a clerkship
was entitled to her month's leave, concluded to
avail herself of it shortly after the Prominent
Official left. Jean, however, who was simply a
Government counter, was not allowed this privilege without losing her pay for each day, or in
fact each hour.

She was looking pale and thin after her illness, and to it was added a great doubt of the
love she had hoped was hers, as each letter from
Ralph became more full of Dora.

When Dora began to talk of her leave, she wrote
to her uncle to ask if she might bring a friend
with her. Having obtained this permission, she
insisted upon Jean going with her. Jean always
tried to save a little ahead of her expenses, and

feeling that she did indeed need a change, at last
consented to go; nor could she have well refused,
for Dora had no sooner conceived this idea of
taking Jean away with her than she began night
and day to argue the point with all her usual
enthusiasm, and Jean finally yielded, she said,
for "peace' sake," although the loss of a whole
month's pay meant many self-denials during the
following winter.

Ralph was delighted with his travels through
the West. He saw Delacy on his way out, and
they decided that, as neither wished to propose
by letter, when Ralph returned to Washington,
Delacy would go with him, and leave it to Dora
to decide between them.

"Absence makes the heart grow fonder," it has
been often said, and thus it was with Delacy.
While with Dora, the confidence he felt in winning her made him at times doubt the sincerity
of his affection for her; away, every one he met
of the fair sex seemed so inferior in beauty and
attraction to him, that he prized what he had
admired in Dora at a higher price than when
with her. Then, too, the uncertainty of what
might happen during his absence to make her
forget him, made him anxious to return and win
her. He had also spoken to his parents about
her, and met with less opposition than he had
expected from them.

Dora and Jean returned from their outing
much improved in many ways. Dora took up
her daily task with less discontent, and in better

spirits than ever. Her month alone with Jean had done her a great deal of good. She was easily led, and what she needed was a firm, true heart to guide her, to help strengthen the good qualities she possessed and overcome the bad ones.

This, of course, could not be done at once. Still, she had become conscious of many of her failings, and this of itself made her more careful of her conduct, but the greatest improvement with her was the cheerfulness with which she resumed her work.

Neither of the girls had forgotten Ralph; but the uncertainty as to who was the favored one, and the many doubts in each of their hearts, had prevented them, even in the close intimacy of their holidays, from confiding in each other.

Winter had well begun when Ralph and Delacy returned. All were delighted to have the young men back, and all seemed to take up the thread of their intimacy just where it had been dropped.

They had been back but a few days when Delacy received from his friend, the Senator, invitations to a great masque ball, of which the whole city had been talking for a long time.

Never had an event of a private individual been so talked of in Washington. The giver had determined that it should be a success as to numbers and magnificence, and had spared no expense to make it such, and the invitations were unlimited. Any Senator or Member or Prominent Official could get as many as he wanted, and thus they drifted down to Delacy.

Of course Dora was delighted with the idea, as she had been longing for weeks to go, having heard so much talk about it. Jean did not like the idea of going to an entertainment of the kind at a house where she was not known, but they all soon talked her over her scruples, and then began to talk of what they should wear. It was too late to think of a costume, so they finally decided upon black dominoes, and Dora suggested that as there would probably be a great many of these, they put some kind of mark upon them, so that if they got separated they could find each other without difficulty.

Jean suggested that, as they had called themselves the "Daisy Chain" on the first evening they had all spent together, white daisies be embroidered upon their black dominoes. To this they all agreed, and all looked forward to having a delightful time together; indeed, Dora was so excited over the idea of going that she nearly made poor Jean sick with a nervous headache on the night of the ball.

The few evenings which intervened, Dora and the young men spent in trying to teach Jean to dance.

Jean would get so giddy whirled around in a waltz, and so mixed up over the figures of the square dances, that they would all laugh until they nearly cried; and such jolly fun did they all have over these lessons that all, except Jean, were sorry when they were over.

Jean must learn to dance, or what was the use of going? Dora would say, and Jean would try, but succeeded only in tiring herself out and making fun for the others. Not that she did not take pleasure in it also, for all were kind in their fun, and she afterwards looked back to those few evenings as the happiest in her life.

When the evening at last arrived, Jean, however, was half sick with excitement and nervousness.

Not so Dora. She seemed to thrive on the excitement, like a tropical plant exposed to the rays of the noonday sun. It was what she loved; what her restless spirit craved. Never had she appeared so bewitchingly beautiful; never had her beauty so dazzled the eyes and confused the brains of the two young men as when they came to escort her to the ball.

Jean, who might have gone as Marguerite, with her fair hair and sweet, pure face, remained unnoticed, while both men stood spellbound before Dora, each anxious to find favor in her sight and be her liege lord at the ball.

That no one was going to chaperone these four young persons may seem strange now, but it was not so then.

So both young men stood waiting to do the honors for Dora, while Jean stood silently by. It was to be a fair fight, they had said, and the lady herself was to choose; this they had again settled on their way up in the carriage. They had both sent flowers to both Jean and Dora, and it had been agreed between them that whose bouquet Dora carried, or flowers she wore, was to be the accepted knight of the evening, and claim the first chance of winning her.

They were both nervous and anxious, as they stood there waiting for some sign from her, that the favored one might go forward and claim her.

Both girls wore simple white dresses, as they had decided not to remain long after unmasking. Their dominoes were of black, with a single white daisy embroidered upon the left breast.

These they threw around them as the young men stood waiting, Dora laughing and talking all the time.

"We are sorry we cannot carry both your flowers, gentlemen, for which accept our thanks, so we have concluded to carry neither; but we can add a few of these daisies to the ones embroidered upon our dominoes." So saying, she pinned a bunch upon Jean and then upon herself.

The daisies were Delacy's gift, and the idea of abiding by her choice of flowers his.

As he stepped forward and helped Dora into the carriage, Ralph turned pale as death, and bit his lips as though in pain. He gave his arm to Jean without a word, and she was so glad to put her hand upon it that she noted not his pale face.

He had searched the town for the finest red roses, remembering she had said they were her favorite flowers. What a fool he had been not to think of a simple daisy, after all that had been said! Daisies at this season were rare, and he had never thought, as Delacy had, of sending to New York for hot-house ones.

Dora and Delacy kept up a steady stream of laughter and jest until the end of their short ride; not so Jean and Ralph—he from the pain and disappointment; she in her nervous antici- pation of the evening.

When they arrived all was brilliant with bright lights and magnificent with gay colors, and odor- ous with the perfume of flowers, with which every available spot in the house was crowded. Gor- geous costumes and flashing jewels, mirth and laughter, and lovely music, met them at the door. Nothing that wealth could produce had been spared; and although the invitations had been given out promiscuously, there were gathered there nearly all the most noted political and so- cial people then at the capital, drawn by the man's great wealth and the political undertow such gatherings often hide.

Of course, Delacy claimed the first dance with Dora, and Ralph and Jean made a poor attempt at dancing.

After the first dance Ralph hastened to Dora to ask for the next dance. When she gave him her programme with a little air of triumph, he saw that Delacy had claimed every round dance and nearly every square one.

Ralph was too inexperienced to hide the cha- grin and disappointment he felt, which he showed by his silence all through the dance, which, being a square one, was all the more noticeable; and although Dora was chatty, she could easily understand that he was hurt. Since the young man's return she no longer doubted whom Ralph loved, as his manner towards her and towards Jean, which she had carefully studied, told its own story. She felt that Jean loved Ralph with all her heart, and if she took him from her she would never know happiness again.

In her efforts to overcome her own will and wishes, like all impulsive people she went to the extreme. She would deny herself this love she felt was hers, that Jean might be happy, and would accept Delacy should he ask her. She did not deny, even to herself, that his position and wealth helped her to come to this conclusion. She liked him, she told herself, almost as much as she did Ralph, and the idea of becoming a rich man's wife was a great temptation to her, especially as she felt that in sacrificing her own love she would make her friend happy. So she had determined to show, this night, her preference, and had done so by bestowing her favors upon Delacy.

They went through their dance almost in silence; and although she felt she had gained her point, she was not happy, and was afraid she would not have the strength to carry out her heroic actions after all, as the following waltz with Delacy failed to repay her, although he was a fine dancer and whispered many a soft, sweet word which should have satisfied her, but which failed to banish from her mind Ralph's silence through the dance.

She felt provoked with herself that her love rebelled and called so loudly for the one she had felt it was so noble to give up to another.

After his dance with Dora, Ralph hunted up Jean. He found her in a bay window, seated on a low divan, where Delacy had just left her, as he hurried to claim his waltz with Dora.

"Please don't ask me to dance," she said, as soon as he drew near. "I have just made a terrible failure with Mr. Delacy, in spite of all my many lessons," she laughed. "It is perfectly delightful to sit here and look at the others."

Ralph was only too glad, and seated himself beside her. He had little to say, but for once Jean paid little attention to his mood. It was satisfying to have him there, and the magnificent and motley assembly claimed the rest of her attention. Dance after dance followed. At last Jean seemed to realize that Ralph was very quiet.

"Do not stay here with me," she said, "because I cannot dance. Go hunt up Dora and enjoy yourself. I shall be perfectly contented and happy here."

Ralph, who was beginning to feel restless, was glad of an opportunity to escape. That he would not ask Dora again to dance, he had determined. She had shown her preference, and he would abide by it. Still, he could not keep from hunting her out in the crowded ball-room, where he found her dancing with Delacy. He stood in a

corner sheltered by some palms and watched her
for some time. On turning to look across the
room, attracted by some slight movement, he was
surprised to see, standing near by, another silent
figure, shaded, like himself, by tall palms, and
clothed in a black domino similar to the one he
wore, with a white daisy embroidered on the
left breast. Who could he be? He stepped out
from his corner to get a better look, when the
silent figure moved quickly away and was lost
in the crowd, and Ralph searched for him in vain.

Dora should have been happy, for she had done
what she wished to do; but such was not the case.
She felt provoked that Ralph had taken his re-
buff so easily, and feared she had denied herself
the pleasure of dancing with him for nothing.
As he did not come near her, she began to think
that he did not care, after all, whether she danced
with him or not. He was probably already satisfied with Jean, and she had been mistaken in
ever thinking otherwise. They were, no doubt,
in some other part of the house, enjoying themselves, and had already forgotten all about her.
She began to feel that she would bitterly repent
the resolution she had made. She was excited
by the evening's pleasure, and she longed to be
friendly with the one she loved. When she at
last saw the silent figure by the palms her heart
gave a bound; she thought it must be Ralph, and
she determined to speak to him. "There was no
reason why she should not have a little enjoyment out of the evening, just because she had

made up her mind to give him up to some one else"; so as soon as the dance was over, she asked Delacy to take her to that part of the room, and then sent him for a glass of water.

She looked around after he had left her, but saw nothing of Ralph, and a feeling of terrible disappointment overcame her.

Suddenly some one stood beside her, just as the music struck up for a waltz. She saw the black domino with the white embroidered daisy, and thought it was Ralph. Before she could speak, the black domino stooped and said in soft, low tones that were almost a whisper:

"Will you dance this waltz with me?"

"Yes," she said, pleased that he had asked her again to dance. He held her hand, which she had placed upon his arm, very tightly, and led her to the extreme end of the long ball-room. Her eyes were fixed upon the floor, and her heart beat wildly as she said, timidly:

"It was wrong to allow Mr. Delacy to monopolize so many of my dances, but I told him at the time that I would reserve the right to break any of the engagements I saw fit."

Without reply he put his arm around her waist and they joined in the dance.

Such a wild dance as it proved to be! It was the last before supper, and the musicians took it in their quickest time. Never had she been so tightly clasped, and yet so lightly glided, as by the silent figure at her side. He seemed to lift her fairly off her feet, and, yielding to the pleas-

ure, round and round they whirled, until Dora,
for the first time in her life, was obliged to stop
for want of breath, and to still the rapid beating
of her heart. Neither spoke for some seconds.
Dora felt confused and oppressed and unconscious of all around her.

"Come with me," her partner said, still in
those same low tones, seeing her confusion and
availing himself of it.

"Had we not better hunt up Jean?" she said,
making one last effort to be true to her late resolution.

"Afterwards," replied he, again in those low,
whispered tones; and not waiting for a reply, and
holding the hand firmly on his arm, he led her,
almost against her will, out of the ball-room,
down the long hall, at the end of which he turned
into a small room with a large bay-window overlooking the garden. This window was open, and
Dora went towards it in delight, to feel the fresh,
pure air once more, after the heated and flower-
laden room they had just left. The hood of his
domino was well drawn down over his mask, and
he stood quietly by while she removed her mask,
and after looking out upon the garden for a few
minutes, and feeling embarrassed by the silence
of the black domino beside her, she said, without
looking at him, and with trembling tones:

"Are you angry?"

Her face had assumed a new loveliness from
the anxiety she felt to know the state of his mind
towards her, a look that gave a pleading, tender

expression to her lovely face, now flushed with the passion of her love and the excitement of the dance.

He did not answer, but slipping his arm quickly around her waist, drew her towards him. Lifting the curtain of his mask, he stooped and kissed her long and passionately upon her sweet mouth. Forgotten was Jean. Forgotten all her good resolutions. Forgotten everything except the blissful thought that Ralph loved her. Hearing approaching footsteps, she freed herself from his embrace.

CHAPTER XXII

WHEN Delacy returned with the glass of water for Dora, he was, of course, unable to find her. It had taken him some time, for the supper-room was now open; and as that was the attraction of the evening to many, it was almost impossible for him to get through the crowd.

He thought that perhaps she was with Ralph, and concluded to hunt up Jean, as it flashed across him that he had paid her very little attention during the evening. He had no difficulty in finding her, as she was still in the seat where Ralph had left her some time ago.

Taking pity upon the quiet little maid, he asked her to go have some supper. They were making their way slowly through the crowd when they met Ralph.

He had taken off his mask, and looked pale and tired.

"Where is Dora?" asked Jean.

"I have not seen her for some time," he replied.

"Where can she be?" added Delacy.

"You danced the last waltz with her," replied Ralph. "Where did you leave her?"

"I have not danced with her since the lancers,

before that waltz. I then left her to get a glass
of water."

Ralph thought of the other silent figure in the
black domino he had seen among the palms, and
wondered what it could mean. He had certainly
just seen Dora waltzing with a black domino
whom he had supposed was Delacy.

"I will find her," he said, and left them
abruptly. Delacy would have followed him but
that Jean was at his side and he had asked her to
supper. He would first find a quiet place for her
and see that she received proper attention, and
then join in the hunt for Dora.

Ralph felt certain that she was with the black
domino; but who was he? Could it be chance
that led him to adopt a disguise in every way so
like their own?

He thought it advisable to search a less
crowded part of the house first, so passed as quickly as he could from room to room; but in vain—
he could see nothing of Dora.

As he reached the end of the long hall, seeing
the bright light through the partly opened door,
he pushed it quickly open and beheld Dora just
as she had freed herself from that long, lingering
kiss.

Ralph could not see her face; but that she stood
there with the man's arm around her, not unwill-
ing, was plain to be seen.

What could it mean? Like a flash, the remembrance of his first meeting with her, and the company she was with, dyed his face with crimson.

It was but an instant that he stood there, when she turned to answer her companion and saw him.

"Ralph!" she cried, and stood dumbfounded, looking towards him and then at the man by her side, who moved quickly past her and out of the room.

Ralph never said a word, but stood looking at her with an expression upon his face she could never forget.

"Ralph!" she again exclaimed, stepping quickly towards him and grasping his arm. "Who is that man?" pointing towards the black domino, who was now outside the door.

"How should I know?" replied Ralph. "It is not Delacy, of that I am sure. I beg pardon for interrupting such a pleasant tête-à-tête," and he turned from her and started towards the door.

"Ralph!" she cried, for the third time calling him by his first name; and laying her hand lightly upon his arm, she looked pleadingly into his face.

Light as was the touch, it detained him. He again faced her; meeting that upturned face, that pleading look, he tried to read her very soul.

For one instant she met his gaze unflinchingly, and then the lids closed over those lovely eyes and the flushed face grew pale as death, and she staggered as though about to fall. The whole effect of her compromising position flashed across her mind, and her shame could well be read as guilt.

Ralph was but human. He could not let her fall, so as she swayed he caught her tightly around the waist, and when once those arms were round her all doubt flew, all else was forgotten except that lovely face so near his own.

"Dora, who was that man?" he now asked of her.

His words roused her, and she quickly moved from the shelter of his arms, and her face was now a crimson flame. She clasped her hands over her eyes and burst into tears, and throwing herself into a chair she sobbed as though her heart would break.

"I do not know!" she cried. "I do not know!"

"Then what was he doing here? He held your hand, his arm was round your waist;' and again Ralph left her side at the remembrance of this and paced quickly up and down the room. For some moments neither spoke; then Dora rose abruptly, her lovely face well up in the air, with the old proud look of tip-tilted chin, and going up to Ralph she stood before him and said:

"Despise me, if you will, but I thought it was you."

"Thought it was I!" Ralph replied, in amazement.

"Yes. After Mr. Delacy left me, to get a glass of water, he came to my side and asked for a waltz. I thought it was you," she again exclaimed, this time not so emphatically, but in a tone that sent a thrill through Ralph's quickly beating heart, "and when after the dance he led me here," she went on quickly, now not looking at him so defiantly, and the proud head beginning to droop, "he hardly spoke a word until we were here, and then—and then——" she stammered, .and now her blushing face was turned away, and only the little crimson ear was to be seen.

"And then——" said Ralph slowly, but with a new light on his face, a new joy thrilling every pulse.

"And then——" he repeated, seeing she had stopped. He put out his hand as though to turn her face towards him once more, but still she moved from him and said impetuously:

"Are you not satisfied? Must I tell you all? Have I not said enough?" and Dora began walking quickly up and down the room, wringing her hands and wishing she were dead, so great was the mortification she felt at thus having to explain herself.

"Dora," said Ralph, going up to her, and taking her clasped hands in both his own, he held her fast.

"Look at me," he continued, seeing her averted face. "Tell me, is it true you thought that man was I, and yet let him make love to you? Is that it? Look at me. Nay, do not hide your face in shame if it be true, for never loved a man truer than I love you. Do not turn away. Was it not so? I saw you by his side."

This last remark was an unfortunate one for poor Ralph, for Dora jerked herself away from his embrace, and all the softness with which the averted face had been filled fled from her.

"Mr. Dennison," she said, with great hauteur, "you need not think it necessary to make love to me because you think I was listening to such love from another, supposing it was you. You interrupted us too soon to know what my decision would be. I might have been listening to such a declaration, but you have no reason to believe that I had accepted it. Now, will you take me to Jean?"

"No, Dora; not until you have listened to me. Things have gone too far between us for me to remain quiet. You must let me plead for myself."

"Do you not think," said Dora, who had now entirely recovered her self-possession, "that you had better go hunt for your proxy?"

"By heavens, you are right! Too much time has been lost already. You know now that I love you. I will be content with that for the present. I will wait for the rest; but it will go hard with that man when I find him."

So saying, they passed out to find Jean and Delacy and then to hunt for his proxy, as Dora had called him. They soon met Delacy, who had been hunting for them.

"Where is Jean?" said Dora.

"I left her in her chosen seat by the window while I went to hunt for you. Where did you manage to disappear to?"

"Delacy," said Ralph, interrupting his friend,

"will you get Miss Hart some supper, if she will excuse me"; and he gave Dora a look which told her why he thus left her, and hurried away.

"Please do not take me in there where all those people are," said Dora to Delacy as Ralph left them. "I am not a bit hungry. I only want to rest."

Delacy was only too glad of this chance, so took her to the conservatory, and finding a secluded seat, he thought that fate had thus been kind to give him so beautiful a spot in which to tell his love. He had noticed the agitation and embarrassment of both when he met them, and he wondered if Ralph had taken advantage of having her alone to try to win her.

That he had not won her consent was evident by his so quickly turning her over to him. This gave him confidence, and thus Dora was again that night listening to words of love.

Dora had been much agitated by the scene she had passed through, and took her seat beside Delacy without thinking of what such a position might lead to. She had not regained her bright, vivacious manner, and her usually animated, rosy face was pale, and the pensive mood so softened her beauty that Delacy had no doubt of his success before he began.

Should the words of a proposal ever be written? Can such words, no matter how well or simply expressed, convey the passion, the delight or despair such words may give when spoken?

Delacy was skilled in wooing, and he had more

than words of love to tell Dora. He had more
to offer than his heart and hand. He possessed
everything to tempt a girl of Dora's character
and disposition—money in his own right; expectations from both father and mother. He was
well enough versed in the ways of the world to
elaborate this part of his story rather than dwell
upon his love.

He told of his beautiful home, his horses, of
the delightful journeys that they could take, and
Dora listened and was tempted. Her present
surroundings—lovely flowers and palms, rooms
of magnificent proportion, filled with every luxury of wealth—appealed to her love of excitement
and fine apparel and the many pleasures wealth
alone can give. All helped to make her wish to
yield; but amidst it all rose Ralph's fair, frank
face, with the love-light she had just seen in his
eyes. Her heart beat too wildly at the remembrance of the scene with Ralph, and the one which
had preceded it, to allow her to yield to the more
calculating part of her nature.

Could she but forget the passionate thrill that
filled her with joy when she first felt that he
loved her, she would gladly have accepted Delacy's offer.

Her face burned with shame when she remembered the mistake she had made; and now, how
could she be sure Ralph had not made his own
declaration because she had betrayed her love for
him ? All her pride arose as this thought crossed
her mind. Sooner than accept Ralph's love, now

that it was mingled with this doubt, she would convince him of his mistake by accepting Delacy.

Delacy pleaded with all the eloquence and tact he possessed, and he was surprised at his own ardor, as Dora's hesitancy made him more anxious than ever to win her.

She could come to no conclusion.

"I am tired and confused over the events of the evening," she at last said. "Let me think of it a day or two."

Although somewhat surprised and disappointed, he could not but consent to this, although he did not lose hope. He still thought she loved him, but did not wish to yield too easily.

"Let us go to Jean; I am very tired," she said, "and wish to go home."

They had walked but a little way when they met Jean and Ralph coming towards them.

As soon as Ralph had left Dora he felt that it would now be impossible for him to recognize the wearer of the black domino, as he had probably thrown it off, and he would therefore have nothing by which to identify him. So, after searching for a while in vain, he returned to Jean, and as the crowd was now much thinner, Jean had enjoyed walking through the many beautiful rooms of the mansion with him. They were just entering the conservatory when they met Dora and Delacy.

"Jean, dear, I am so tired," Dora said; "I want to go home."

"Want to go home! Well, you surprise me,

I thought I would be the one to beg for that, and that you would want to remain until broad daylight."

"Well, as I have told you before, I am not to be depended upon."

"You are indeed pale. No wonder—you have danced too much, while I have been sitting still most of the evening. Come," and both girls went into the dressing-room for their wraps.

Little was said on the way home, and Dora, who had started out so gay, was the quietest one there, while Jean had the most to say. She alone of the four had thoroughly enjoyed herself. Ralph had spent most of the evening by her side. She had been extremely interested in watching the others, and she alone had enjoyed the splendid supper. Though not a gourmand, such delicious things to eat she had never even imagined, and so, satisfied and happy, she chatted all the way home.

CHAPTER XXIII

"Are you too tired, little blossom," said Dora that night, coming into Jean's room in her dressing-gown, and her lovely hair falling in thick waves over the white dress, "to talk a little before going to bed?"

"I never felt less like sleep," said Jean.

One of the luxuries of Jean's room was an open grate. The fire there was burning brightly, and Jean, lowering the gas to a dim spark, drew up a big arm-chair and seated herself therein. Dora threw herself upon the large bear-skin in front of the fire—a mammoth skin which had been given to Jim by a fellow clerk, who had brought it from the far West. When Dora was restless and nervous at night—as she frequently was—Jean could nearly always soothe her by brushing her hair and gently rubbing her forehead, and so it was no unusual thing for Jean to seat herself in the comfortable chair, while Dora would lie at her feet, and be mesmerized into a state of drowsy sleepfulness, at peace with herself and the world.

> "Idly they talked of waltz and quadrille,
> Idly they laughed, like other girls,
> Who, over the fire, when all is still,
> Comb out their braids and curls."

But that night Jean did most of the talking at first. Finally she began to wonder at Dora's silence, and so for quite a while neither spoke. All of a sudden Dora began to sing in an undertone one of Burns' quaint old songs:

> " 'Lady Mary Jean
> Was a flower i' the dew;
> Sweet was its smell
> And bonnie was its hue,
> And the longer it blossomed
> The sweeter it grew;
> For the lily in the bud
> Will be bonnier yet.' "

She raised herself upon her knees, and, taking Jean's face between her two hands, kissed her on both cheeks and said:

"Now, Burns was thinking of just such a Jean as you when he wrote that, I am sure."

Still on her knees before Jean, and with the bright fire at her back, she sang the second verse in soft, low tones:

> " 'Young Charlie Cochran
> Was the sprout of an aik;
> Bonnie and blooming
> And straight was its make;
> The sun took delight
> To shine for his sake,
> And it will be the brag
> Of the forest yet.' "

She stopped and looked intently at Jean's face, and felt sure that the bright color there was not all due to the firelight. From the time that the black domino had taken her into that room until she had arrived home she had forgotten Jean in the whole matter, and the good resolution she had made to yield Ralph to her. Now that she had listened to Ralph, and knew of his love for herself, she felt it might be a surrender in vain. She felt perplexed, confused, and knew not how to tell her friend of all that had passed, or how to decide for herself, so she had come into Jean's room to decide upon some definite plan of conduct.

"Now, I don't know 'Young Mr. Cochran,'" she continued, still looking intently into Jean's flushed face, "but all the way home I could think of nothing else but this verse."

"With a tall, handsome young man by your side, you could not think otherwise."

"Do you think that was it?" said Dora. "I wish I could be sure." She said this very seriously, and again resumed her old position on the rug, with her face toward the bright fire, and hands clasped round her knees. Not waiting for Jean to reply, she added, quickly:

"Mr. Delacy asked me to marry him to-night."

"Oh, I am so glad," said Jean, leaning over and kissing her pure white brow, now devoid of all bangs and lovely in its fairness. She did not turn her head, but said:

"Are you? Why?"

"Because I think he is very fond of you, and he is very rich—and——"

"Oh, saucy Jean! Who would think you so mercenary as to think about riches in connection with so sacred a thing as marriage? After all your preaching!" And Dora shook her finger at her in mock surprise.

"You know, Dora, that if I did not think he was a nice young man the riches would be nothing to me. There are some natures that need the luxury of wealth to make their lives complete. You are such a one. You are like a beautiful diamond, lovely at any time, but most perfect when suitably mounted and surrounded."

"And you are like the flower in the dew. No golden mounting could make you more beautiful or add to your lovely nature. If I am like a diamond, as you say, I have also its hard, cold heart, its sharp edge, its changeful lights. Of what good is the brilliancy and beauty if it only leads me astray? How can I ever be happy when, with the veritable power of the stone you say I resemble, I cut and wound my dearest friend?" and Dora hid her face in Jean's lap.

Jean was startled at the serious view Dora had taken of her simile.

"Do you not love him?" she said, gently, thinking she referred to Delacy.

"Whom?" said Dora, again raising her head and looking at Jean.

"Why, Mr. Delacy, of course. Were we not talking of him? I think he would make you a good husband. Did you refuse him?"

"No," said Dora; "neither have I accepted

him. It is too good a chance to throw over lightly. I like him and the riches are an attraction, and yet I hesitate."

"Like is not love, dear," said Jean, "and you of all women should marry for love."

"I do not know why you say that, I am sure. I would make a very bad wife for a poor man, with my hatred of work and all my extravagant ideas."

"That is just it. Love alone will keep you in the right path, and the man you marry for wealth may some day find himself without a cent. Then what would poverty be to you? Marriage is not for a day, a week or a year. It is for life; and the wisdom of man has decreed that the vow we take to consummate that event contains the clause 'for better or worse,' and nothing but love can make us live up to that vow. It is not a festival at which we are to dance and enjoy ourselves forever, but a serious Mass in which prayer and praise must alternate with much preaching, penitence and tears. I am sorry you do not love him, for with love and wealth your path would probably be among the singers of joy. Are you sure of your own heart, dear?"

"Yes," said Dora, almost in a whisper.

For a while both were silent, both looking into the fire, each afraid to speak their thoughts.

"Dora," said Jean at last, "why are you so sure?"

Dora shivered and buried her head in her knees. Jean saw the shiver, and as the room was getting cold, she arose, and getting a soft white knitted shawl, threw it around Dora's shoulders. As she did so, Dora drew her down upon the rug beside her, and holding her close to her, put part of it around Jean also.

"We are both under the same 'cloud,' dear," she said, as she wrapped the other end around herself. "I have a confession to make, dear. I know why you made that mistake at the office, but I never could bring myself to tell you from what it saved me"; and Dora told it all, and how and why she had forgiven the Prominent Official. As she spoke of how she had renewed the intimacy with him, it flashed across her for the first time that the black domino must have been he in disguise.

Step by step he had regained the ground he had lost, until she had become convinced that he had repented of his conduct in trying to get her to go alone with him to Baltimore, and that he had no longer aught but the most respectful friendship for her. She was not one to bear malice, and, after all, he had only told his love and had never asked for aught save her friendship. It is hard to blame others for loving us, and she became convinced that she had taken offense where none was offered her, and had put a wrong construction upon his words. Having once given him an opportunity to plead his excuses, he was enabled, by skillful flattery, to regain her tolerance at least. She became rather ashamed of her own hasty action, as his politeness towards herself led her to believe that the evil intended was all of her own imagination.

She remembered now that he had spoken about the ball, and she had said she was going, and had told him the disguise they were to wear. Not until this conversation with Jean did she recall all this; the confusion produced by Ralph's appearance had paralyzed her memory.

Now she stopped in the midst of her confession to think of this, to realize that through it all he meant her harm. She was interrupted in this thought by Jean's saying:

"What you should have done, Dora, was to have gone right to the chief, shown him the letter and he would have protected you, and the Prominent Official would have been prevented from renewing his acquaintance with you. I am so sorry, dear, but as it was for my sake, I will not scold you; but, please, I beg of you never to speak to him again. He will only get you into trouble, and I am afraid harm will come of it now."

"It has—oh, it has!" said Dora. "I paid for it to-night. I fear it has spoilt my whole life," and her voice and face told the misery she felt.

"What else happened to-night? You have not told me all," said Jean, and she took the lovely head and laid it on her shoulder. "Tell me all, dear; perhaps I may be able to help you."

What could Dora do but tell her all? Pillowed on the heart she knew she was breaking, she yet had not strength to keep back all that had happened—all! Yet her suffering was keen, and sharp as a serpent's tooth, as she felt that slender form quiver and shrink as she told of Ralph's love, until she could stand it no longer, and arose and walked the floor.

"But I will not marry him, Jean—never, never! He does not really love me; he only said so because he is so kind, so self-sacrificing, that he thinks it necessary, now that he believes I love him. I will write and accept Mr. Delacy the first thing in the morning."

The words Jean strove to speak seemed to freeze on her lips, and the pain at her heart seemed greater than she could bear, and she sat as though stricken dumb. At first she seemed only half conscious that Dora came to her, and, resuming her seat beside her, kissed her on the brow and said: "I will never marry him, dear, and he will find out after all that it is you he loves."

At last Jean aroused herself with a mighty effort and said:

"What are you saying, Dora? Do you think I would accept such love? No! He loves you —I have felt this for some time—and he will not lightly turn from that love to another. Oh, you do not know the love you are turning aside. He is young, unformed in many ways; but, as you said awhile ago, he will be the pride of the forest yet. You will be proud of him, and he will make you happy; do not let false pride ruin both your lives." Jean started in rather weakly;

but as she realized the situation, she grew eloquent and proved to Dora that she, who could so praise the man she loved to another, would have strength enough to refuse the second place in a man's heart, and deserved a much better fate.

Before they parted that night, or rather morning, Dora had promised Jean to accept Ralph, should he again speak to her of love; so she at least went to bed, if not happy, in a much more contented frame of mind than when she had returned from the ball.

Jean sat alone before the fire until near the break of day—sat with sorrowing heart at the funeral of her dead hopes.

A sorrow that was as sweet as joy. No anger to weep over; no deception to bewail; no love grown cold; no sin to regret. Only, the pure, sweet love for him, which had sprung in her heart unsought, unknown, must be buried and forgotten, if she could. How could she blame him if he had passed her by when he had once seen Dora?

> "Thou art rose-lined from the cold
> And meant verily to hold
> Life's pure pleasures manifold.
> I am pale as crocus grows
> Close beside a rose-tree's root:
> Whosoe'er would reach the rose
> Treads the crocus under foot."

And then she told herself, how could she grieve over what she had never possessed? and yet, life

would never be the same again. Some hearts
there are who answer to each love that is offered
to them through life, if only through sympathy;
while others bestow all of which they are capable
upon one, and can awake to the touch of no other.
She was like a beautiful fruit-tree, which, from
the abundance and beauty of its first fruit, be-
comes thereafter a barren tree; with the warm
spring breezes there come only soft green leaves;
no bud or blossom can be seen—it stands erect
and tall in an orchard of plenty, but yields no
profit but shade.

She finally arose and walked to the window,
and looked out upon a pure white world, with
a faint tint in the east, which told of the rising
sun. It had snowed fast since they had returned
from the ball, and trees and lamp-posts and all
projections were heavily laden with the soft
Southern snow—snow that so soon turns into
slush and mud; snow that drapes each bough and
object with such voluminous folds, and with vo-
luptuous grace covers all the earth with the light-
est, softest touch, as though grieved at the harm
it might do; and so, striking as lightly as possible,
lacking the hard, cold glitter of the North, it soon
passes away in tears.

As Jean looked out upon the snow, she felt
that over her had passed a mantle, changing the
form of her life, and hiding out of sight all
that had made life so sweet to her for many
months,

CHAPTER XXIV

ON their way to the office next morning Jean made Dora promise that she would go to the Chief of the Bureau, and tell him all that had passed between the Prominent Official and herself. This she did, and it was not long before that person was closeted in the little office which was built over the stairway, receiving the severest talking to he had ever had in his life. In the afternoon he received a long envelope containing the information that his services were no longer required, and thus he was dropped out of Dora's life.

If Dora and Jean had talked until late in the night, Delacy and Ralph had also compared notes, and neither knew just what to think. Delacy claimed that she must love Ralph, or she would not have listened in the way she did to what she supposed were words of love from him. Ralph said if she had loved him she would not have hesitated to refuse Delacy.

Both were perplexed; but, unlike the two girls, they did not confess their inmost feelings to each other. All they could do was to wait until they should hear from her. They had not long to wait, for the next afternoon Delacy received a note from her thanking him for the honor, etc., but she felt sure she did not love him enough to become his wife.

Of course he felt cut and hurt at this refusal; but the wound, as we know, was not deep, and he had many ways of soon forgetting it. He was sincerely fond of Ralph, and was glad that he, at least, and no other, was to win her, as he now believed. He lost no time in letting him know of her decision, and wished him success in his wooing. He would go East, he said, immediately, as he had some clews to the heirs of the estate over which he had so long been working. He would keep Ralph posted as to his whereabouts, and Ralph must invite him to the wedding.

Ralph felt that if Dora had refused Delacy, with his wealth and position, it must be for love of him, and he determined to lose no more time in finding out; so, as the snow was still on the ground and the sleighing passably good, he hired the best sleigh he could get (which was not saying much) and was at her door that evening. The smooth concrete streets allow a thin covering of snow to make sleighing possible, and people in Washington have to take it as they can get it, and dare not wait for better, for a few hours may bring slush; therefore, the Avenue was gay with the jingle of bells, and handsome and elegant sleighs rushed side by side with the most grotesque vehicles on runners—old sleighs that had been packed away in barns or stables, rusty, paintless, and broken, now made splendid by old army blankets or bed-comforts, drawn by anatomical studies of horse-frames, resplendent with clanking cow-bells, and occupied by muffled figures with heads tied up in old shawls and feet in ragged carpet. Anything and everything that could be put on runners, from packing-boxes to high-top buggies, were out racing up and down the broad Avenue; while on the sidewalk promenaded, to watch the carnival of sleighs, fully as mixed a crowd—cabinet officers and senators, foreign diplomats and scientists mingled freely with clerks, mechanics and negroes.

Ralph and Dora were soon among the gay sleighers; but as Ralph was anxious to have a few words of vital importance with Dora, he soon turned into a more quiet street, and in a little while had told Dora all about the love in his heart, the plans and hopes of his life. He had a good paying position, with which he was delighted, as it took him most of the time from place to place, and allowed him to see much of this great country.

As he had thus far had but little experience with the confinement of office life in the Department, and his work was new and pleasing, he was, of course, enthusiastic, and thought little of the slaughtering and dismissals every change in the Administration brought.

When Dora had confessed her love, he pictured to her a beautiful life. They would travel together through the West, from one Land Office to another, and then be called back to Washington to remain for awhile, until he would be or-

dered off again. This idea of going from place
to place was very attractive to Dora, and the future seemed filled only with the most delightful
anticipations of journeys and changes—things
that she dearly loved; therefore, the picture as
wife of a "Special Agent" in the General Land
Office became a most desirable one to her.

It is needless to say that the next evening
Ralph was again in Jim's cosy parlor, receiving
the congratulations of his friends, and from none
more sincerely than from Jean.   Jim and Marie
had felt a little disappointed when they had first
heard of the engagement, as they read Jean's
secret, and were anxious for her happiness; but
as they saw her cheerfulness and ready entering
into the plans of her friends, they thought that
they had been mistaken, forgetting that—

"Hopeless grief is passionless."

When Ralph heard from Dora the part the
Prominent Official had taken in her life, his
indignation was mingled with a fear that out of
revenge for her having been the means of his dis-
missal he might seek to do her future harm;
he therefore began to plead for an early marriage and the right to protect her.   He dreaded
the idea of being sent away from her, and as
there was no real reason for delay, they decided
to be married early in the spring.   All the same,
he did not delay long in hunting up that "gentleman," and what passed between them will not be
forgotten by the Prominent Official at least.

So when the trees were in blossom, and the early spring flowers peeping from the young green ground, Dora and Ralph were made man and wife.

It was a very quiet affair, as both Dora and Ralph had few friends in the city, and Ralph was to take Dora to his home after the wedding.

The "Judge" came down to "give away the groom," he said. Delacy really came to the wedding. He "had one great desire," he said, and that was to kiss the bride. Ralph had won her fairly; but if he would allow him this privilege, he would forgive him.

When he saw Dora a blushing bride, in her simple gray gown, and the big bunch of tulips which Jean had given her in her hand, all the old longing returned, but he had to make the best of it, and find consolation where he could, in the free and easy life of a rich young bachelor.

Dora's uncle, the Rev. John Hart, came down to perform the ceremony, which took place in Jim's parlor, amidst green palms and boughs of apple-blossom which formed a bower over the heads of the lovely bride and handsome groom.

After the ceremony Delacy created a sensation by asking what she meant by being married by one name, when they had all known her by another.

That was easy to answer, she said. Her mother's maiden name was Hart. Under this name she had made a reputation before her marriage as a singer. After her husband's death she had

returned to the stage and her old stage name.
As it complicated matters in many ways to have
her child known by a different name from the
one by which she was known, she had brought
Dora up under the name of Hart. Of course,
when she married she took her full name of Dora
Hart Price.

Delacy then asked her uncle for full particu-
lars as to her father, Mr. Price, and his ante-
cedents. Mr. Hart having told him all he knew,
he told them that he was uncertain, but felt convinced from what he heard that Dora must be
the heiress he had been looking for so long. If
so, he congratulated them both, for the fortune,
he said, was a large one.

By the time Ralph and Dora returned from
their wedding journey, Delacy had found all the
necessary proof, and Dora soon had all her heart
could wish—the husband of her choice and a
large income.

Ralph resigned the position for which he had
fought so bravely—and, after all, the best thing
a young man can do after obtaining a Government position is to resign it before it ruins him,
for any business career he may afterwards have
to seek—and gave all his attention to the study
of law. Because he had unconsciously married
a rich woman he did not intend to remain idle.

They went West after receiving his diploma,
where he soon built up a large practice; and true
to his old ambition, he took an active part in
politics, and it was not many years before he was

sent to represent his adopted State in Congress, and you can see and hear him now if you come to Washington while Congress is in session.

Dora's new position and ample means gave her plenty of excitement; and as she had learned her lesson before marriage, she was able to fulfil her duties with grace, beauty and tact, and within the limits of "what the world said."

Often as she drives with her elegant teams up Executive Avenue, she glances up to the windows where her face used so often to be seen, and she feels like Lamb did when he wrote of seeing the "shade of some dead accountant, with visionary pen in ear, flit by, one by one, stiff as in life."

She often thought of how near she had been to the edge of the precipice, and she never forgot the good friend who had taken such an active part in shaping her life. She frequently recalled the afternoon she and Jean had gathered daisies on Meridian Hill, and she realized that on that day she crossed the dividing line of her life, and when she came to Washington she always had Jean with her in her lovely home as often as Jean would come. She and Ralph had both pleaded with Jean to resign her position and make her home with them for life, but Jean said, "No, she could not give up her position of 'a Government Countess.'"

Mrs. Graham had married the Senator, and they frequently met in official life, as the Senator was a man who stood very high with the Administration, so that it was impossible for them to avoid meeting; but their former acquaintance was never resumed, although Mrs. Graham made many efforts to have it renewed.

In the course of time Marie, by much self-denial, and much urging of Jim, was enabled to make the first payment on a little home in Mount Pleasant, and almost before they knew it the little home was their own, and is now greatly increased in value.

For many years Marie had been happy with her little family around her, and free from the worry of Jim's being dismissed without cause, since the clerks had been put under the protection of the civil service, until the cry arose, "Put the old clerks out!" "Make places for the young men!" But, worse than all, there has arisen the specter, long thought dead, of peremptory dismissals without appeal.

When Jim thinks of this he blesses his little wife, who induced him to secure a roof over his head, if the axe should at last fall.

Jean took up the even tenor of her way ere this beautiful "bird of passage" fluttered in among them. Life was not just the same, but her nature was so sweet and gentle, so pure and unassuming that life would always hold something beautiful in view and her heart find out some generous deed to do. She still makes her home with Marie, and her delight is the little garden that makes their home beautiful.

She is like a little faded white rosebud, and she will tell you that it is "better to have

loved and lost than never to have loved at all,"
because of the sweetness of giving, and in her
diary that closed "her eventful year" she wrote
the thoughts which are as true to-day as they were
then:

Hope has fled, but love remains,
And pains and sorrows it disdains.
The leaves have fallen from the rose;
The stars shine, but the bright sun goes.
Hope has fled, but love, so dear,
Sheds no tear o'er leaves grown sere.

For the fallen petals disclose the seeds;
From these can never grow wild weeds.
The stars reflect the glory of the sun
And cheer us when the day is done.
Though love's to-morrow can never be,
To-day I'm happy in my love for thee.

And yesterday, and the day before,
Love still reigns, though hope be o'er.
Farewell, sweet hope; you led me on
Until the perfect seed was won,
And planted deep within my heart—
The brilliant bloom and leaf alone depart.

The little seed, the germ divine,
Like a glorious star at night doth shine.
What though it never blooms again,
'Twill bear no thorns to give me pain.
Yes; hope has fled, but love divine,
Nourished in memories, still is mine.